WHEN ELEPHANTS FIGHT

Majok Tulba was born in South Sudan and came to Australia in 2001. His first novel, *Beneath the Darkening Sky*, won the 2014 Kathleen Mitchell Award, and in 2013 was shortlisted for the Dylan Thomas Prize and the Commonwealth Book Prize. He was named one of the *Sydney Morning Herald*'s Best Young Novelists of the Year in 2013. Majok is the founder of Okay Microfinance, a social enterprise launched in 2016 that aims to improve education for girls and community health, and to find sustainable solutions for families to break free of the cycle of poverty in South Sudan. He lives in Sydney with his wife and children.

ALSO BY MAJOK TULBA

Beneath the Darkening Sky

MAJOK
TULBA

WHEN ELEPHANTS FIGHT

HAMISH HAMILTON
an imprint of
PENGUIN BOOKS

HAMISH HAMILTON

UK | USA | Canada | Ireland | Australia
India | New Zealand | South Africa | China

Penguin Books is part of the Penguin Random House group of companies whose addresses can be found at global.penguinrandomhouse.com.

Penguin Random House Australia

First published by Penguin Random House Australia Pty Ltd, 2018

10 9 8 7 6 5 4 3 2 1

Cover design by Alex Ross © Penguin Random House Australia Pty Ltd.
Cover photographs: Shutterstock: Melissa King/Shutterstock.com; Orlok/Shutterstock.com; Thongchai Pittayanon/Shutterstock.com. Getty: Carsten Koall/Getty Images.
Typeset in Adobe Cason Pro 11.75/17.5 by Midland Typesetters, Australia.
Printed and bound in Australia by Griffin Press, an accredited ISO AS/NZS 14001 Environmental Management Systems printer.

NATIONAL LIBRARY OF AUSTRALIA

A catalogue record for this book is available from the National Library of Australia

ISBN: 978 1 92642 843 7

penguin.com.au

FSC www.fsc.org MIX Paper from responsible sources FSC® C009448

For those who inspired it

Part One

1

My older brother, Deng, doesn't live with us anymore. I don't know where he went. He's been gone a long time now but my heart still aches when I come home and he's not there. Sometimes I make out he's hiding behind the bushes, waiting for me to find him like in the old days. But he isn't, and I know he's not hiding anywhere nearby, no matter how hard I pretend. I know he's far from our village of Pacong. Some nights I dream I'm walking with him across a valley of tall green grass beyond the hills.

I've asked Grandpa if he knows where Deng is but he doesn't like talking about it. As my father is dead and Grandpa is getting old, it's up to me to bring our family back together.

Thiko tells me I have to keep believing I will see my brother again. I must never let go of that hope, she says, and her voice is always kind. Thiko is my good friend, even though she's a girl, and I try to heed what she says. But I find it hard to hold onto hope at times, it feels so slippery.

At school she and I sit in the same row, Thiko on the far west side of the room, me on the east. Our classroom is made of mud walls with a thatched roof and everyone who gets to sit inside it and learn is proud to be there. From the window I can see children from the lower classes under the trees. I used to sit under those same trees when I was younger and didn't know how to write with an ink pen. I'd look over to this window, the one I'm looking out of now, and I'd see Deng. He would wave or smile and I'd wave and smile back. I didn't even have to look at the window to know he was there, I just always assumed he would be.

I can also see the office of our teachers from here. This morning we're waiting for Miss Ayen. My class has sixty boys and ten girls, but you wouldn't know it from the noise level as we wait. You'd think it was the other way around. The girls are so loud I can't stand it.

'Can you please be quiet?' I shout to no one in particular, and a short chubby girl with a round face and bright eyes sticks her tongue out at me. Another throws a pencil. I duck and it misses my head, just. The rest go on yelling and laughing.

'They sound like weaverbirds having a fit,' says Chieng from the row behind me.

I turn and agree with him. Chieng is small in frame but he's tough. Last year he bit the ear of a bully, and didn't stop until his lower and upper teeth met through the flesh. When he finally let go, the screaming victim ran straight home to his mama.

Chieng is always making jokes, about the girls, the teacher. The only girl he doesn't joke about is Akol, who moved to our village not long ago. She lives on the road leading down to the Nile. Chieng follows her around like a puppy, brings her squirrels after a hunt. It makes his day when Akol thanks him or gives him a smile. He likes to believe she thinks he's a superhero. Without Thon-gool, my dog, I don't catch squirrels anymore. I curse the Sudan People's Liberation Army who killed him.

The girls quiet down when Miss Ayen comes in to give us English dictation. She walks up and down the rows of desks as she reads from her book. I try to pay attention but Chieng nudges me.

'Hey Juba,' he whispers, low enough that Miss Ayen can't hear. He isn't intimidated by her, even though she's stern and serious about learning. Chieng is not so serious about learning. He likes to fool around whenever he can, and sometimes this is fun and I join in, but mostly I want to learn.

'Hey!' he whispers, louder this time.

I wait until Miss Ayen has walked past and then, as I turn, my forearm bumps my ruler off my desk and sends it clattering to the floor.

Chieng fights laughter. Miss Ayen stops reading and she stops walking for a moment, still with her back to me. Everyone else stops writing, pencils mid-air. All eyes are on me except Miss Ayen's. She hasn't turned around yet. I want her to turn around. I want to see her expression.

'Sorry, Miss Ayen,' I say, leaning down to retrieve the ruler. But my hands feel like they've been greased and the ruler keeps slipping from my grasp. It clatters to the floor again. Chieng laughs, doing his best to be silent about it.

The third time I drop the ruler it falls in such a way I can't reach it from my seat. I must stand up to get it. I scramble out and kneel on the floor and try to grasp it with both hands, but it's a wild animal with a mind of its own. Chieng lets loose with a snort of laughter.

'Shh,' I hiss at him.

Miss Ayen only turns around once I'm finally back in my seat. Her face is expressionless but I can tell she thinks I've done this whole thing on purpose. I take up my pencil and glue my eyes to the paper. The silence in the room is like smoke.

'Come here, Juba,' she says at last, and her voice is calm.

She has returned to her desk and is waiting for me. I put my pencil down and slink up. Even though my back is turned to the class, I can feel everyone watching. I'm wondering what Thiko is thinking. I'm embarrassed to know she's looking at me right now.

'I'm sorry, Miss Ayen,' I say. 'I wasn't trying to be disruptive.'

She studies me and says evenly, 'Whether you were trying to or not, interrupting a dictation is not something I take lightly. Is it fair to your classmates, who are trying to concentrate?'

I lower my eyes. 'No, Miss Ayen.'

'You know the rules, Juba. Bend over and touch the desk.'

I do as she says, keeping my eyes on the worn surface of her desk. No one, except maybe Chieng, silently once more, is laughing now. They are all glad they're not me.

Miss Ayen's red rubber rod zings as it moves through the air. I grit my teeth. The first hit is always startling, even when you know it's coming, the second is the one that hurts most. My eyes water but I blink it away. I don't want my classmates to think I'm crying. The third hit hurts a bit less, partly because my backside is already going numb. I blink again, my jaw clenched. None of us boys want to cry in front of girls. Miss Ayen has never whipped any of them, even though they deserve it the most.

We were all surprised when Miss Ayen appeared in our classroom for the first time. We didn't know women could be teachers. I thought she must be lost when I saw her standing in front of our class. Nobody got up and greeted her, like we do male teachers, and there was no reaction as she introduced herself.

'Tell me your names,' she said. 'Starting from here.' She pointed at a thin boy sitting in the corner but he just stared at her with a stunned expression on his face. 'You don't know your name?' she asked him.

There were murmurs and giggles from the other boys.

'Well,' said Miss Ayen. 'Which of you can tell me your names?'

Thiko raised her hand, and soon the rest of the class did likewise. That day we found out that females could be teachers too. Eventually we learned they could be great teachers.

At the end of today's class Miss Ayen asks me to stay behind for a minute.

'Sounds like you're in trouble,' Chieng whispers as he makes his way out of the room. 'Good luck.'

Even Thiko casts a worried look in my direction as she files out, but Miss Ayen smiles as I walk up to her desk.

'You're not in trouble,' she says, and my shoulders relax. She reaches into her desk drawer and pulls out a well-thumbed book. 'This is for you,' she says.

Really? A reward for being punished?

I take it from her. '*Winnie-the-Pooh*,' I read. 'What is that?'

'It's a childhood book of mine. One of my favourites. Pooh is a foolish bear much of the time,' she says.

My heart squeezes. Is she comparing me to a foolish bear?

But as I flip through the pages I'm drawn in. 'Can I borrow it?' I ask.

'It's a gift, Juba, one I hope you'll enjoy.' She looks at me as if she feels a little guilty. 'You know I have to punish everyone equally, but in fact you're my best student. Certainly the best at English. It's a pleasure having you in the class, most of the time. You can take this book home and share it with your brother and sister. You're a great example for them. My hope is that they'll see how much you love learning and will come to love it too. Pooh may be a silly bear in the main, but he has a heart of gold and he's loyal, he loves his friends. I see these qualities in you. The difference is, you're a lot smarter than he is.'

Knowing the bear has a heart of gold lights my heart, but at first I don't want to accept Miss Ayen's gift. I'm still mad at her for whipping me. My backside is aching. Teachers don't whip their favourite students. But not accepting might give her another reason to whip me, because I'd be refusing to do what I'm supposed to be doing as a student, reading. Then I think how Miss Ayen wants me to learn, and that's a good thing. So I thank her and take the book, cradling it like a treasure as I go to join the rest of the class for geography.

When I was a small boy, before I attended school, I thought the River Nile and the sun and the tallest trees of Pacong were the boundaries of the whole world. But our geography teacher tells us stories about other countries and the endless seas and oceans that surround them. I love geography, but I'm looking forward to breakfast once the class is over, because every day I wake up at four am, or sometimes five when there's no moon. I work in the garden until six o'clock, then have a bath and clean my teeth. At half past six I take the goats to the fields, and leave for school at seven-thirty.

Our classes start at eight o'clock, and we have two before breakfast, at ten. We can eat this wherever we want. Chieng and I used to have breakfast at the base of a tamarind tree. I would wedge myself between its leafy branches and watch the never-ending blue sky. It made me think of impossible things, like climbing trees so high that I could touch the clouds. But lately I eat with Thiko.

There's shouting and laughter as students stream off to breakfast like chickens being released from a cage. The dust makes my nose itch as though an insect is crawling inside. Thiko and I go to sit on a log at the edge of the yard and I show her my book. I won't show it to Chieng, I don't want him to make fun of me and call me teacher's pet.

'What was that in English class?' she asks. 'You should know better than to mess around with Miss Ayen.'

'I wasn't doing it on purpose. Chieng was trying to tell me something and when I turned to look at him I knocked the ruler off. Then it became the slipperiest thing ever and I couldn't keep hold of it.'

Thiko smiles. 'It *was* kind of funny.'

Well, if it made Thiko smile, it was worth it. Even if it did get me whipped.

Thiko's family came to live in the village about five years ago. Before that they lived in a cattle camp northeast of Pacong, three hours' walk away, where they looked after cows. Cattle are like gold and currency in South Sedan. You're nobody in our tribes if you don't have a cow. I don't have one. I never liked cows. My father had fifteen cows and a great fat brown bull. He was proud of his cows, although his herd was nothing compared to those people who own hundreds. He took me several times to the cattle camp when I was young, but it was no fun for me sleeping beside the smelly cow dung under the moonlight, covered in ashes to ward off mosquitoes.

Maybe I'll have to buy some cows one day, when I grow up and am ready to marry. Our tribe has a saying: no cows, no wife. Or maybe a rich man with a lot of cows will marry my little sister Nyanbuot, and I won't have to buy any at all.

Thiko's father didn't want her to go to school at first, but when all the family's cows were raided by a rival tribe and there were none to look after, they came to Pacong. Once they were here, her mother convinced her father to allow Thiko to go to school, and I became friends with her.

That came about when I was sitting with Chieng at lunch one day and a group of girls approached her. They looked like a pack of wild dogs closing in on an injured zebra. I could see that one of the girls had a pair of scissors in her hand.

'What are they doing?' I asked Chieng.

He glanced up and went back to his lunch. 'Who knows? I don't try to figure out what girls are thinking, it's a waste of time.'

Just as he said this, one of the group grabbed Thiko's braid and the girl with the scissors snipped it off. Thiko let out a cry as a third girl yanked her head round the other way and the girl with the scissors went after her again. Thiko squirmed away, but the scissors nicked her forehead and it started bleeding.

'They're going to hurt her,' I said, getting up and going over, even though I knew I'd be subject to endless ridicule for saying something to these girls. 'Hey, stop that!' I yelled.

My shout brought Miss Ayen running up, and the girls scrambled to deny they had anything to do with the blood, or the braid that lay on the ground. But they were ordered to spend the rest of the day sweeping the courtyard.

'Are you okay?' I asked Thiko.

She wiped the blood off her face. Her gaze went sadly to the braid on the ground then back to me. 'Yes I am, Juba. Thank you. Thank you for helping.'

I thought of how most girls would be crying about that lost braid, but Thiko did not. That day, I walked her home from school, and her mother offered us food. Thiko's father was already sick then, and he died not long after. Thiko doesn't have brothers or sisters and she and I became good friends from then on, and the gang of girls stayed clear of her.

This morning's breakfast is roasted sweet potato. Thiko and I eat looking out at the assembly field, where boys are kicking around a football and raising dust. None of them really know how to play properly, they mainly pretend. The sun glows in a cloudless sky.

Bol, an older boy one class ahead of me, leaves the field and walks towards us. He's muscular and has a thick neck, and likes running into others on the field and making them go flying. If a victim complains he laughs like a satisfied hyena.

Now he gestures to me as if he wants to tell me something. I put my breakfast down and go over and straightaway he pushes me. I stagger backwards but manage to stay on my feet.

'Hey, leave me alone,' I say.

Bol moves closer and jabs a finger into my chest. 'I'll leave you alone when you leave Thiko alone.'

Thiko jumps up. 'I want *you* to leave Juba alone! He's never done a single thing to you.'

Bol grins and gives me another shove. My mouth goes dry. I don't want to fight him but I don't want him to think he can go round picking on me, even if he is older. And what's his problem with Thiko?

Across the yard I can see Chieng talking with Akol. If I could just get him over here we could fight Bol together.

'Why don't you bother someone your own size?' a new voice says.

It's Majok, who's taller than Chieng and me, the same height as Bol.

Bol looks from Majok to me and back to Majok. 'This doesn't have anything to do with you,' he says.

Majok smiles and turns like he's about to walk away, then he spins and kicks out with one of his long legs and catches Bol right in the ribs, keeling him over.

Bol scrambles back up and threatens to tell his teacher. Majok laughs. He's the blacksmith's son, and he's smart and charming and can do no wrong in the teacher's eyes. If he gets in trouble today, it will be his first time. He shrugs away my thanks and Bol slinks off.

When they've both gone Thiko says, 'I don't know why older boys are always so mean.'

I think back to when Thiko had her braid cut off. 'Girls can be just as mean,' I say. 'But still, I should have fought him.' Part of me is glad I didn't, but a bigger part wishes that someone else didn't have to take care of the situation for me.

'He's taller and bigger than you,' says Thiko.

Perhaps she's trying to make me feel better, but I want to be able to stand up for myself. Then I think how if Deng had been here, Bol wouldn't have done anything in the first place. And that makes me want to rescue my brother from the rebels even more.

No one has said that's where he is but I have a feeling. South Sudan, which is what we call where I live, is at war with the government, which is in the north. Men in South Sudan who don't like the government of the north join the rebels and fight for independence. Grandpa has told me that the war has been going since 1955, although it stopped for a while in 1972 and started again in 1983. So I was born into war.

Deng witnessed the killing of our father by government forces, and I believe he might have joined the rebels to avenge his death. Chieng and I have gone to distant villages to ask after Deng but no one has been able to tell us anything.

Breakfast over, we gather at the entrance to our classroom to wait for the maths teacher. He's not like our other teachers, who prefer to come in and find their students already seated and quiet. The maths teacher likes to be the first to enter, then he'll turn around and count us in like goats.

I'm standing in line with Thiko, Chieng and Majok. 'Did you do your homework, Juba?' Chieng asks. His voice tells me he's done his.

'I tried. I couldn't do it. I can't do maths.'

'Yes you can,' Thiko says. 'You're smart.'

'He's not smart at maths,' Chieng says with a grin.

The teacher arrives clutching textbooks in one hand and a thin brown cane in the other. He walks briskly into the classroom and we file in after him. Once we're all in our seats he returns our homework.

I close my eyes as he places mine before me. When I know he's gone I open my eyes to see a big 'F' in red pen. I put my head on my desk.

'Juba, come up here please,' the teacher calls.

Chieng and Majok are beaming with pride and Thiko gives me a worried look. None of them struggle with maths like I do. The rest of my classmates look at me with knowing eyes: I'm the only one who has failed the assignment. I drag myself to the front of the room.

The teacher pulls the cane from behind his desk. I put my hand out and hold my breath but he pauses and stares into my eyes, as if he's forgotten what he's supposed to do. Maybe he'll let me go, I think, and I breathe again. But next minute he brings the cane down on the back of my hand. I rub my skin to try to ease the stinging and the class roars with laughter.

'Next time I'll hit both hands,' he says. 'Now return to your desk.'

I wince as I walk back, my hand throbbing and everyone's eyes on me. How can I have been hit twice in one day?

Maths is the longest lesson but finally it's over. The teacher leaves and we wait for Miss Ayen to come and teach us history. She should be here already. She's always on time, but the minutes pass, the classroom grows louder.

I'm looking out the window when I see two men walking towards her office. One has a gun strapped across his chest and he takes long, proud strides as if he's the king of the world. My heart jumps. They're Sudan People's Liberation Army rebels.

Miss Ayen gets up from her desk when she sees them coming. I stand on my toes for a better view. Chieng and other students are looking now too. The men say something to Miss Ayen and she sits back down and puts her elbows on the desk, rubbing her brow as if she has a headache. Then she opens a drawer and hands them money. The man without the gun takes it, counts it, and stuffs it in his pocket with a satisfied grin.

Luckily this must be the only thing they came for, because they leave. Miss Ayen stays at her desk, her face tight. At last she gets up and walks across the yard to our classroom.

We're all back in our seats when she comes in holding textbooks to her chest as if they're babies. We stand as she enters. She says nothing, waves to tell us to sit. Normally she'd greet us.

Her hand shakes as she writes on the board and the chalk snaps. She keeps turning to look out of the window. I can see that she's sweating, like she's been walking in the hot sun.

When school is over for the day I leave with Thiko. It's sunny and birds are singing in the trees. At the sound of a twig breaking and the rustling of leaves I hold my breath. I know it's foolish, but for a moment I hope it's Deng coming out of hiding in the bushes.

2

Under the mango tree near our hut I can practise my maths in the dirt. I don't want to fail the next assignment. When the sun cools down I go to work in our garden. This is the best time of day for outside work, in the magic hour when the sun dyes everything gold, before creeping behind the woven mat of branches and leaves like it's shy. The scent of the moist earth makes me feel alive. Green flies play music on the droppings of a small animal, a fox perhaps. I don't mind those droppings, they fertilise the crops.

On this side of our garden we grow groundnuts, kidney beans, sorghum. Pacong is known for having the best groundnuts, because of its sandy soil. When we have excess we sell them in the market, and they're transported to villages that don't grow them. The planting season is April to June. July is weeding season, and late August to December is harvesting season.

Planting and weeding are hard work because the gardens in Pacong aren't small. Some are as large as five acres and we do everything by hand. The whole family joins in the planting, even Grandpa, although he's getting too old to weed, too old for the sore ankles and aching knuckles. At harvest time, Grandpa and Mama give the first of the produce as an offering to the Lord in church.

Pacong is beautiful. Mahogany trees and tall palms line both sides of the main dirt road that passes through the village. From this road, paths curve off into each neighbourhood, like the veins on Grandpa's hands. Our huts are mud with grass-thatched roofs. Near the centre of the village, where my family lives, they're closer together, but further out they're wide apart, with room for farming. Beyond the village, the main road winds over the hills and through the trees. It's orange dirt, cracked and potted with holes that turn into puddles in the rain. The River Nile is twenty minutes away, and everywhere there are streams flowing from it.

Our geography teacher told us that about twenty-five thousand people live in Pacong. A large fig tree marks the village meeting spot where the Paramount Chief leads the councils. He's a respected man, and Grandpa says he's well known all over South Sudan. The chief has two hundred and fifty sons and a hundred and ninety daughters, from nearly ninety wives. He spends most of his time solving matters under the fig tree.

A horsefly distracts me from my work in the garden. It buzzes past my ear and settles on my cheek. I slap at it just as it pierces my skin. The pain blinds me for a moment but I know I'll be okay. It's not like the sting of the scorpion I stepped on last year. That made my muscle cramp and I cried for two days.

I chop the hoe into the soil and feel the air change. Dark clouds slide over the lowering sun, filling the whole sky. Thunder rattles. Then suddenly the rain comes and I drop my hoe and run as fast as I can to our hut. There's a slick of mud outside the door and I slip and fall. From the doorway Thon, my little brother, laughs.

I scramble to my feet and run inside, slamming the door behind me. My shorts and T-shirt are heavy with mud.

'Change your clothes,' Mama says in the kitchen, 'or you'll catch cold.'

The cooking fire has sucked up all the fresh air, making it hard to breathe. I open my mouth and inhale like a fish. Except when it rains, we cook in the open kitchen outside. Thon cries whenever he gets smoke in his eyes, and only cries louder when I tell him not to be a baby. Nyanbuot is helping my mother cook dinner. She loves helping with the housework. There are little beads of sweat on her arms and face in the sweltering hut.

Our hut stands inside a circle of four palm trees, and off to the side is another hut for the goats and chickens. Ten chickens and a big red rooster, also a small white rooster that likes to practise crowing when the big one isn't nearby. The hut is close enough for us to hear if there's any trouble at night. I keep a fire burning permanently to protect the goats from hungry hyenas, and the chickens from wild cats. I sleep in there sometimes, when we have important visitors.

My family's hut is really just one big room divided into three by a low mud partition. I share a bamboo bed with Thon on one side of the hut, with a mat that needs replacing, and Nyanbuot and Mama's bed is on the other side, covered with a piece of dyed cloth. Mama had to sell a goat to buy her bed but I made mine myself. In the centre of the hut sit three carved wood and bamboo stools and a small table with a broken leg, which I bound with string. The smoke-blackened kitchen is behind this area.

The storm is a strong one, it's making the walls of the hut vibrate and I'm afraid it may break them. Rain pounds the roof as if the sky is flinging arrows at us. It's male rain. I don't like male rain, with its thunder and lightning. Female rains are soft and gentle.

With clean clothes on I sit by the window and watch what's happening outside, where everything is enveloped in a grey haze. The grass at the edge of the yard is dancing wildly, bats are swaying from branches, leaves are falling. Clouds curdle like bad milk in the heavens and the wind whistles and hisses in the palm trees.

I can hear hyenas howling somewhere, a sound that always sends shivers down my spine. They prowl the village at night, sometimes coming into huts looking for prey. When that happens I call Grandpa to come with his spear. Old as he is, he fears nothing. But right now he'll be in his own hut with his wife, Yar, who we call Momo. Our real grandmother died young of an unknown disease. Momo is nice, and I like the smell that spikes the air when she cooks fish. Grandpa never leaves her side. They don't shout or yell at each other, not like our neighbour who fights with his wife every night. Grandpa used to run in and break them up but he doesn't bother these days.

At last the rain slows to showers and the storm clouds fly away to the north. After eating dinner I lie on my bed and listen to the music of rain. The next thing I know the cock is crowing and it's morning. I'm late.

I walk outside and brush my teeth quickly with a brushing stick. I've been using this stick for a month now and it's getting shorter. I'll get a new one after school today. I go back into the hut, grab my schoolbag and bolt without saying goodbye to Mama. I don't always like how she fusses with my hair and clothes and tells me to take care. I'm not a baby anymore.

Mama doesn't want Thon to go to school because there'll be no one to take care of the goats. Mama says that if I become important I'll be able to buy cows, and Thon will take them to the cattle camp and look after them there. Grandpa doesn't want Nyanbuot to go to school either. He says she should stay home until a man can pay a good dowry for her.

My feet bounce on the dusty road as I walk and I keep myself busy practising maths problems with my fingers. Thiko is running ahead with some other girls, her schoolbag dangling on her back. Chieng and Majok join me on the way and we arrive together.

There's a car outside the school, which means Waterman is here. He must be bringing more supplies.

Waterman is white. The first time I saw him I wanted to touch his pale pink skin to make sure it was real. I wasn't the only one who felt that way. All the kids chased his car as he drove through the village, we all wanted the chance to touch him because his white skin looks like an illusion.

For a while I thought Waterman himself wasn't quite real, that he was a dream we all shared. And in fact he is something of a mystery to us. Where is he from? Why is he here? I mean, I know he's here to bring supplies to our school, but why isn't he in his own country? His car was the first to ever come to our village. It made us feel like we lived in a big city.

I still haven't touched Waterman's skin but by now we all know that he *is* real. Today he's got textbooks, exercise books, and boxes of pens and pencils and coloured chalk. I'm not sure where he gets this stuff from but he always seems to have a large supply.

The last time he came he was with two white women, nurses who gave out oral polio vaccines in the village. Waterman told two boys and a girl it was not the work of a witchdoctor that caused their legs to feel like they had no bones in them, it was polio.

We don't have a clinic or doctor in Pacong. If people need to clean a wound they boil tree roots and leaves. Once, a woman in the village had paracetamol tablets sent by a relative living in a distant country, but they quickly ran out. So the parents of the children with polio went to see a powerful witchdoctor, who instructed them to kill two white and two red roosters and put their feathers behind the huts, and in two corners inside, to cure the disease. It didn't work.

So when the nurses came with the vaccine, many women lined up with their children. Chieng, Thiko and I helped to translate, because the mothers speak only Dinka. After the women had gone home, the nurses asked us to have a picture taken with them. We stood in a group and Waterman took the photo.

'Smile,' they said. I didn't want to smile, but thinking about being asked to smile when I didn't want to made me smile anyway as the camera clicked.

'Beautiful,' said Waterman.

Now he's busy talking with two of the teachers, but he nods at us as we walk past. Everyone is always happy to see him, especially the teachers. Even Miss Ayen clamours for Waterman's attention, laughing at his jokes and thanking him profusely for whatever he's brought. We all look at him with admiration and I wonder how that must feel, to walk through a village and know everyone in it appreciates you deeply.

The school bell rings. We take our bags into the classroom and come back outside to sweep the compound. The yellow and orange disk of the rising sun is brightening over the sky. Miss Ayen is supervising. She's wearing her rainbow-coloured shoes today. I don't know how many pairs of shoes she owns. Sometimes she comes in with shoes that make her look as if she's walking on her toes, and I wonder how she can be comfortable in them.

Many students stop work when she looks away or goes over to the other side of the yard. Some of the kids have brooms that are too big for them. They chase each other around, dragging the brooms behind them, kicking up dust, making even more of a mess. Dust wafts into my throat, my nose, my eyes.

'It's sad when you have to have a *girl* stick up for you.' Bol's voice comes from right behind me. I turn and immediately feel his hands on my chest, shoving me backwards.

'Are you growing any balls yet?' he snarls. 'Let me check.'

He moves to grab my genitals and when I push his hand away he slaps my hand and squeezes my balls hard. I gasp for air.

'Do you think your balls are big enough?' Bol's face looks so ugly right now.

'No,' I whimper. 'My balls are small.' I glance around, trying to see if anyone is looking. Miss Ayen is nowhere in sight.

'Good,' he hisses. 'I don't want to see them grow.'

'Okay,' I squeak.

He loosens his grip and I swallow air as he strolls off. My legs are wobbling. I feel like I'm about to crumple to the ground but I steady myself. I don't want anyone to see me on my knees because of Bol, even if the pain is excruciating. I'm already ashamed of letting him play with my balls like marbles.

The muscles around my groin strain and pull as if they're trying to move my balls to a safer location. Maybe I should scream. I open my mouth but stop myself, letting the air out and gritting my teeth instead. The pain might go away if I stop thinking about it.

I go back to sweeping. My muscles start to relax and the sun feels good. I close my eyes and let the rays bathe my face, but then suddenly Bol is back.

'We didn't finish our conversation,' he says.

'I don't have anything to say to you,' I tell him and he shoves me again, hard enough this time to make me lose my footing.

A satisfied look flashes across his face. This is what he wanted, to prove he was stronger than me.

'I don't care if you have nothing to say to me. *I* have something to say to *you*. And that is to leave Thiko alone. I don't want you talking to her anymore. Understand?'

I get to my feet. 'I understand you want to bother me for no reason at all.'

'Are you stupid? Just stop talking to Thiko. Stop liking her.'

So that's it.

'I don't like her like that,' I say. This isn't quite true, but what business is it of his? 'She's a friend,' I add.

'Sure. That's why you're always following her around like a dog. Because you're her *friend*.'

I try to ignore the way my heart is thudding against my ribs. I remember Deng telling me once that it doesn't matter how much bigger your opponent is, you must be brave and stand up to him. But I don't know what it means to be brave. How many times can I tell Bol to leave me alone? And how can I tell Thiko I don't want to be friends with her anymore because Bol ordered me to?

'If Thiko doesn't want me to talk to her,' I say, 'she can tell me herself.'

'Ha!' Then he appears to consider something. 'I'll tell you what, Juba. If you want me to leave you alone, beat me in a game.'

This is a surprise turn. 'A game? What game?'

'Wrestling.'

'I don't know how to wrestle,' I say. Chieng, Majok and I have messed around a bit but there's no way I could beat Bol at wrestling.

'Then whatever, any game. That's how much confidence I have that I'll be able to crush you into the ground. Doesn't matter what game it is.'

The only thing I can think of at this moment is a foot race, and seeing as I'm the fastest boy in school, I should win. But I wouldn't be surprised if Bol tried something dirty, like tripping me up or taking a short cut. Before I can even suggest a race, though, he shoves me so hard I go sprawling.

He's on top of me before I have time to move. I put my arms up to cover my face and deflect the blows from his fists. It's all I can do. If I try to get a hit or two of my own in, it will leave my head vulnerable, and Bol wants nothing more than to break my nose and give me two black eyes. He sits on my middle and punches me in the throat. I stop breathing for a second.

Over the sound of Bol's heavy breathing, I hear other noises. And then a loud voice, Miss Ayen's.

'Stop this *now*!'

The punches cease. My mouth is salty. There's dust in my eyes and all over my face. My arms throb. Majok and Chieng are pulling Bol off me, and Miss Ayen is yelling at him. A crowd has gathered around us.

'This type of behaviour will *not* be tolerated,' Miss Ayen says. 'Bol, I'm sending you home for the rest of the day. I'll come later to talk to your parents. I don't think your father will be pleased to hear you've been causing trouble.'

Bol scowls in a fury but says nothing.

I stand up, brushing myself off. In the crowd I see Thiko looking worried. I'm glad she didn't rush over to help me. I'm glad I at least got up on my own. Miss Ayen is looking at me too, and for a second I think she will send me home as well, but instead she tells me to go and clean myself up.

The students return to their sweeping as Bol heads one way and I go the other. I do my best to clean the blood and dust off my face using the pail of water by the entrance to our classroom. The inside of my cheek stings when I touch it with my tongue. I can feel a small hole there. I must have bitten it when I fell.

Some days I think it might be better if I didn't come to school at all, but I like being here and I like learning. I don't even mind maths that much, I'm just not any good at it. But knowing there's someone out to get me makes it a lot harder to enjoy school. I'm not sure what I can do. I'm not a skilled enough fighter to beat Bol. And he's been in so many fights before. Most boys just do what he says. I can't imagine having to hide every time he turns up, and I don't want to live in constant fear that he'll try to hurt me.

I take an extra long time washing. I don't feel like talking to anyone, even if they want to tell me Bol is a bully and deserves to get sent home. At least I won't have to worry about running into him for the rest of today.

When I'm done I go back to sweeping. Most of the girls have abandoned their brooms completely and gathered in groups, arms linked. They're making faces, whispering one second and laughing out loud the next. They act like they're at a party. Part of their conversation drifts over towards me with the dust – they're talking about the boys they think are cute. I hear my name, followed by shrieks of laughter. I don't know if the laughter is a good sign or not.

But I have little time to think about it because there's suddenly another sound, a deep rumbling in the air like a plane. A flock of birds flies from a tree, moving as one mass, first this way then that. The rumbling grows louder and I scan the sky for the plane, hoping it's one of those that leave white trails behind like a ribbon unfurling.

I imagine the passengers on such a plane. People going someplace where they will spend their days relaxing, having fun. I can't really picture what that would be like, but I've heard that's what some people do.

There is no plane, or at least none that I can see, only the clouds. I look around, but no one else seems to have noticed the sound. Chieng is talking with Akol. Aliens from outer space could land right next to him and if Chieng was with Akol he would barely notice. Thiko is nowhere in sight. The sound is buzzing in my head. How is it that no one else has heard? I want to scream at them.

And I do. It's bloodcurdling, the scream of someone who's lost a limb. When I run out of breath and stop, my throat feels raw. Everyone is staring at me as though I've gone mad.

Then two things happen at once. Miss Ayen appears on the far side of the yard with a ruler in her hand, and my schoolmates look up at the sky as they finally hear the noise. It's right above us now, and there's a new sound too, a whistling, whooshing sound I've never heard before.

Miss Ayen yells, 'It's an Antonov!' and before we can blink there's a rapid *boom boom boom* and the earth groans as if suppressing pain.

The ground heaves beneath me, a bucking zebra trying to throw me off. Another explosion follows quickly, a high buzzing sound, and I drop to the dust under a tree and wrap an arm around the trunk, anchoring myself as best I can and biting down on my lip until I taste blood. I remain there, eyes closed, my fingers gripping a root, until I feel brave enough to open one eye.

I can't believe what I see. The school buildings are in rags of fire and smoke. Trees have become pillars of leaping red, and flames gust out of the ground ahead of me. Dust boils towards the heavens. Everywhere there is noise and panic, students howling, feet stampeding. Not far from me, two boys lie curled on the ground, covering their ears with their hands.

My whole body feels like it will explode. I want to run as far away from this as possible, but fear paralyses me. I cannot move.

Then I see Thiko. She's out in the middle of the compound, in the smoke and flying debris, just standing there like a living ghost, immune to danger.

That's enough to make my limbs move. I get up and run, dodging airborne objects. I trip and fall, spit out dirt, and when I get back up Thiko is gone. I call out to her and get no response.

I turn to keep searching and my eyes land on a body lying on the ground in a pool of blood. God, no, I can't be seeing this, I'm imagining it. I blink and look again.

It's Akol. Her eyes are open but she's not seeing anything.

Oh God, please. This is a bad dream, it will end, like all bad dreams eventually do. I close my eyes. When I open them again everything will be as it was. The bombing will not have happened, we will be sweeping the compound, Miss Ayen will be on duty.

But when I open my eyes Akol is still there. Motionless. As if she's playing a prank on me and will get up any minute, laughing at the look on my face.

I am about to go to her when someone rushes past me. It's Chieng. He collapses at her side. Screams louder than I've ever heard anyone scream. Then he shakes her, gently at first, but when she doesn't move, when her eyes don't lose that blank stare, he shakes her harder.

'Akol!' he sobs. He has her blood all over him.

'Chieng.' I take his arm. I want to talk to him to stop him losing his mind, I want to pull him away in case there's another bomb, but he pushes me with a force that nearly knocks me over.

I grab him again, tighter this time, and manage to get him to face me. 'Chieng, listen to me, she's gone. We have to get out of here, it's not safe. She's gone, Chieng.'

'I can't leave her,' he cries, but his body goes slack and he allows me to pull him away and through the compound. I try not to hear the screams all around us. I try not to look. I don't want to see any more dead bodies. I want to find Thiko and go home to Grandpa and Mama.

Then, miraculously, as Chieng and I round the corner of a deserted hut behind the school compound, we run straight into Thiko. Relief floods her face when she sees me. She's covered in dirt and dust but there's no blood. She's okay. She is here, dirty and scared and okay.

'Thiko,' is all I can manage to say, and she grabs my hand, the one that's not holding Chieng, and tugs me away, out through the low shrubs bordering this edge of the compound.

There's a body here, another there, and another. Students who a short time ago were laughing, sweeping the yard, playing around. I don't understand how this is possible. I can't wrap my mind around how everything has so suddenly changed, how the air that was clean and fresh is now full of smoke and chaos and terror. I step on something warm and wet and almost trip over something harder. I want to believe it's a log. I feel dizzy. I would have fallen if I wasn't holding Thiko's hand.

A boy I don't know lurches up to us, a wild look in his eyes.

'Please help me,' he sobs. There's a gaping hole in his shoulder where his right arm should be.

I grimace. If those white nurses were here they'd know what to do. But there's no one here to help us, and before Thiko or Chieng or I can do or say anything, the boy collapses. His eyes roll back in his head and his body twitches. I look away.

Then, something even worse. We come across Miss Ayen's

shoes. They're not rainbow-coloured anymore, they're stained dark with blood. A few yards beyond them are two long legs, unconnected to a body. The bright white of the leg bones shines through the charred flesh. I try to look away again but I'm not quick enough. My entire body goes rigid. I keep walking but I don't feel as if I'm walking. The image is seared in my mind.

My lungs seem to be filling with water, there's no space for air. I can't feel my legs at all now. I want to cry and I don't want to. I don't know what to do. A part of me is trying to get away from my body, trying to escape to where the trees are tall and the grass is soft. I can't tell if I'm stepping on solid ground or off the top of a mountain. Everything around me is a blur of red and noise.

And then, the part of me that wants to get away does. The screaming stops. The pain stops. The whole world stops.

3

When I open my eyes the ceiling is familiar. The mat beneath me is familiar. Mama is standing beside my bed, staring down at me. A smile begins to form on my face. It *was* all a bad dream. The bombing, the dead bodies, Miss Ayen's shoes.

But the look on Mama's face makes my smile disappear before it can surface. She sits down and takes my hand. Pain courses through me. My head throbs. I try to remember what happened, how I made it home. I struggle to sit up but I'm too light-headed.

'Be careful,' Mama says.

'Where are Thiko and Chieng? Is Majok okay?'

'They are all safe,' says Mama, easing me back down on the bed. 'They're unhurt. A branch struck your head, Juba. But there's no bleeding. You'll be alright.'

Thon and Nyanbuot are hanging back with scared eyes. I put my hand to the back of my head. It's swollen and sore to the touch and feels as if there's liquid inside.

'We must pray,' Mama says. She folds our hands together and we close our eyes, and she offers up a prayer for the wounded and those who lost their lives. I try to listen to what she's saying but my mind fights it. Terrible images explode behind my eyelids.

'And Lord,' Mama says, 'I give my most humble gratitude for sparing the life of my son.'

Her prayer brings me little comfort. I do not want to thank God, because I don't understand why he's let this happen. Grandpa has said many times that there's no sense in war, but I don't think I really understood what he meant until now.

Chieng and Thiko and Majok come over later and sit quietly beside me. There's not much we can say, there are no words for what happened. Then Grandpa comes back in and checks the lump on my head. He asks Mama to boil some herbal leaves in water, then leaves again and returns with a razor blade and a piece of cloth. When he asks Chieng and Mama to hold my arms down I get agitated.

'Let me do it,' says Thiko.

Grandpa looks at her and shrugs. Thiko puts her palms on the backs of my hands and I relax. I know deep down that I have to let Grandpa help me. When he slices the lump with the blade it bursts and blood flows down my neck. He dips the cloth in the herbal water and presses it on the wound. I can feel the pain all through my body, right down to my toes. I focus on Thiko's eyes and the little beads of sweat on her nose, grateful that she's unhurt.

When Grandpa is finished, Mama wipes the blood off and takes the cloth and bowl away. Grandpa sits back and looks at each of us, one by one. He stays like that for a long time.

'You are all lucky to be alive,' he says at last. 'I know it might not feel like that now, but over time you will see how fortunate you are.'

I look at Thiko and Chieng and Majok and we nod together. We do know we're lucky.

But Chieng's grief is deep. 'I close my eyes and all I see is Akol,' he says, and his voice is barely a whisper. 'I should have protected her. I should have, but we got separated and . . . and . . .' He cannot finish his sentence.

Thiko puts a hand on his arm. 'You can't blame yourself,' she says. 'And at least Akol knew how much you cared about her.'

'But *why*?' Chieng asks Grandpa. 'My mother told me it was a government plane. Why did they do this?'

Grandpa sighs. 'I don't know,' he says simply. 'Who can really know why such evil happens? But I could say that the government wants to send a message to villages they think might support the rebels, by attacking what's most precious to them, their children. You know, the north can't afford to let the south become an independent country.'

Grandpa has explained this to me before, how the government of the north needs our resources. They have used the oil that's here in South Sudan to develop their part of the country, and they don't have to depend on international aid like we do.

Grandpa goes on, 'When the British governed Sudan as a colony, they administered the north and the south separately at first. North Sudan became Arabic-speaking, because Egypt was also in there. After the British left, Arabic was made the language of administration in the south too, so northerners began to hold positions here.'

'But I don't speak Arabic,' Chieng says.

'No, of course you don't. But the southerners have been kept out of their own government even when they're educated,' says Grandpa. 'The rebels say they're fighting not just for political and economic independence, but also religious freedom. The north doesn't like our Christianity, they want to impose Sharia law.'

Grandpa looks sadder than I have ever seen him. I remember him telling me once that government forces are stationed in many towns in South Sudan, including Rumbek, just thirteen miles from Pacong.

When my friends have left, Nyanbuot brings me food I cannot eat. All I want to do is go back to sleep, but I keep seeing Miss Ayen's shoes. I talk to the ceiling. The noises from the explosion ricochet around my head. Thon comes to stand over me and asks if I know why the fire fell from the sky. I tell him to ask Grandpa.

Eventually I sleep. In the morning the swelling on my head has gone down a bit, although it still hurts. I get up as the sun is rising and go to sit on top of my favourite rock, a hundred yards or so from our hut. From here I can see the narrow path leading to the waterhole, the path that leads to the market, and the wooded area where I collect firewood.

Every season the view from this rock is different. In spring Pacong is a sea of colourful leaves. On dry-season nights, when all the crops have been harvested and stored away, the village comes alive with cooking lights, as though someone has taken a handful of glitter and sprinkled it over the huts under their blanket of black sky. One night, Chieng and I tried to count the stars and were lulled to sleep by the warm breeze and the songs of crickets.

This morning, aside from the wind, there's no sound. No one is working in their garden or sweeping their yard, no boys are herding goats to the fields. Pacong is completely silent. The sky is low with a scattering of thick grey clouds. Today they seem to me like pieces of an impossible jigsaw puzzle.

Miss Ayen's hut is not far from ours, and I can see people gathering there. Family members will arrive throughout the day, from distant villages. As I watch, some can't control their emotions, they throw themselves on the ground, beating their chests in grief. One of her sisters strikes the dirt wildly with her palms until I am certain they will bleed. She is howling like an animal caught in a trap, a sound that's coming from other parts of the village too. Mama told me that thirty students are dead and many others have been injured. I don't know whether any other teachers were killed.

I get down from the rock and then go with Mama to pay our respects at Miss Ayen's house.

'We must pray for her family,' Mama tells me. 'She took care of many of them, and now that she's gone they cannot be sure how they will get by.' Because of the war, Mama says, many things are scarce in parts of South Sudan, and Miss Ayen used to send her family money, soap, sugar and salt.

I had never considered this before. I'd never thought about what Miss Ayen's life outside school might be like, about how many people depended on her. I think of the book of Winnie-the-Pooh and I want to cry again.

Outside Miss Ayen's home a car pulls up. It's Waterman. He's with two other white men and his face is hardened when he gets out. I don't know if there's something he can do about those responsible for the school bombing.

Today is the first time I haven't seen people flocking to him. Waterman talks with Miss Ayen's family while the other men place bags of food and jerry cans of water in the yard. Then he comes over to me and says they're going to rebuild the school. It will be even better than it was before.

'I don't understand why they bombed it,' I say. 'Why would anyone want to bomb a school?'

Waterman rubs his chin for a moment, as if he's unsure what to say. 'Some people don't care what they destroy, I guess.'

He seems reluctant to talk more about the bombs. But I know Waterman isn't one of those people who like to destroy things. He could probably have any kind of life, but here he is helping us.

'We appreciate everything you've done for us,' I say. 'Even if the school doesn't get rebuilt.'

'Oh, but it will be rebuilt, Juba, I promise you that. All children deserve an education. You must never lose hope.' He looks me in the eye. 'This isn't something you can be half-assed about, you know. Hope will keep you strong, even when everything else deserts you.' Waterman's voice is thick with passion and determination.

I want to ask him why he cares so much, why it matters to him that we have a school, but I don't want to be rude. I don't want him to think I'm ungrateful, or that I'm questioning why he's doing all this for us.

And suddenly I wonder if the school was targeted because the more people learn, the more they will know there is something wrong with the government, and then they might want to join the rebels. But I know the rebels are no good either. They kill people too, take our food. I don't know whether they took Deng or he wanted to go with them.

Once Mama and I have spoken with Miss Ayen's family, I head to Grandpa's hut, which stands behind large tamarind trees. On hot afternoons I love to play in their shade and listen to the whistling birds. The bamboo fence encircling the hut is falling apart in places.

Momo is cooking fish soup. I sit down and talk to Grandpa. I've been thinking about what he told me yesterday, that the bombs were dropped by pilots from the government of Sudan. I had always wanted to be a pilot when I grew up. I would put my arms out to the side and run around the yard yelling, 'Pilot. I'm a pilot.' It felt good the way the word formed in my mouth, the way it popped out, *thuok tiera*, every time I said it. I imagined myself as a grown man and people asking me what I did for a living, and me saying, 'I'm a pilot. I fly planes above the clouds.' I really believed I was going to do that someday, and whenever I said so, Mama responded the same way, saying I had to study hard. I got through many school lessons by telling myself I was going to be a pilot.

But now, I tell Grandpa, I don't want to be a pilot anymore.

He looks sad again when I say this, and tells me there's still plenty of time to decide what I will become. To take my mind off things he gets out his mancala board and we play for several hours.

Later that afternoon, Chieng joins me on my rock and we sit with our legs hanging over the side, looking out over the village. I'm amazed by the transformation. Where this morning Pacong was silent, as if nothing would ever be the same again, now people are working in their gardens, talking and going about their business. Birds are singing, the flies are out and biting. The sky is vivid blue, dotted with puffy clouds like sheep in a heavenly pasture. It all looks so peaceful that for a moment it's hard to believe what's happened.

Chieng hasn't talked much since the bombing. He just looks stunned. But I know his mother has been very kind. She is a beautiful and hardworking woman, while Chieng's father is lazy and leaves most of the work to his wife and Chieng and his two brothers and three sisters.

Their father's saving grace is his singing voice and his skill as a dancer. Chieng has told me that this was how his father won his mother's heart. Now his father spends most of his time composing songs for the men in the village. He says that any man who owns a beautiful bull with a red nose, a black and white hide, and a white patch that shines like a star on its face doesn't work in the garden. I don't believe him. Many people in the village have beautiful bulls and they still work in the garden.

Because we are boys, I'm allowed to go and sleep at Chieng's house if I want to, and he's allowed to sleep at mine. Girls aren't allowed to do this. But I go home to sleep that night. Except I can't find sleep. As soon as I lie down my heart feels like a hunted gazelle. I listen to Mama's breathing in the dark, and the slow breath of Nyanbuot. Lucky them. Thon twists and turns. I wonder if he's having bad dreams. Branches scrape against the side of the hut and I imagine bomber pilots outside, trying to get in. It's the wind, I tell myself. That's what Mama always says.

After a while I give up. I get out of bed, grab a stick and steal outside into the darkness.

A cluster of stars hangs above like ripe fruit and the moon beams down as I walk the path through dew-soaked grass to Grandpa's hut. I know he will still be up, he always goes late to bed. I watch my steps, swiping my stick from side to side on the ground in front of me. The night is alive with sounds and movement, and the breeze is soothing, like the caress of Mama's hand. I stop for a moment to enjoy it, and feel better until a fox darts across the path and sends my heart into my throat. An owl flies close beside my head, the wind from its wings catching my ear.

I find Grandpa sitting by a small fire in his hut with his legs folded beneath him. He doesn't close his door sometimes because he says he likes fresh air. Momo is snoring softly on her mat on the other side of the hut.

'It's late, Juba,' he says softly. 'Why have you come?' The sound of his voice is soothing as always, even if it still seems a little sadder than usual.

'I can't sleep,' I say. Creeping into the moonlight from the window, I settle beside him, and he tells me a story about when he was in the church choir as a child. He performed for the bishop, he says, and was nervous for days.

'We were dressed in our choir clothes. White shirts and black trousers for boys, white shirts and black skirts for girls. And red vests with three crosses on them, two small ones and a big one. We got divided into two groups, a line of boys standing on one side of the path and a line of girls on the other, from shortest to tallest. Then we heard voices. They were coming. The bishop, the ministers, the pastors and priests.'

'How many of them?' I ask.

'Over five hundred.'

I stare at Grandpa in awe.

'They went into the church and we followed. The congregation stood when we walked in and sang our hymns. It was wonderful, Juba.'

We talk until I finally drop off, and I wake to a milky orange light spilling across the room as the sun peeks at the land.

Back at home our goats are crying. They haven't eaten for a day and a half. Because of what happened, Thon is afraid to tend the goats on his own. I release them and herd them into the fields. A bee-eater rides along on one of the goats. Another chases a grasshopper and soon a large flock have gathered overhead. Under the trees the sunlight is dappled and makes me feel safe. For a moment I even forget about the bombing.

I try to imagine what Deng would do if he was still in Pacong. Before he left, it was his job to look after the goats. He took me with him sometimes, and the big boys would order us young boys to run after the goats for the whole day while they played. Goats keep moving from one place to another and it's impossible to watch them all at once. I have got better at it but it's still not easy. Sometimes they refuse the grass and run off into someone's garden, where they eat the groundnuts or sorghum. I have to try to get them out while the garden's owner shouts at me. During school breaks, Chieng, Majok and I often tend our goats together. It's more fun that way and less lonely.

When I come home Mama is pounding sorghum with a stick, to separate the grain from the stalk. She winnows the grain in the wind to get the dirt out and then grinds it into flour on rough grindstones. Some days, when she has the time and is not tired, she washes the grains after separating them and pounds them in the mortar and pestle. This way the outer part of the grain comes off and can be used in making the local beer, or given to goats. Then she grinds the white inner part of the grain, the best part. Mama sings as she does all this. They say in our village that if a woman isn't singing while she does the housework, she isn't doing much work at all. Maybe singing makes the long process easier.

While Mama grinds, Nyanbuot shells groundnuts, then fries them in a pan and pounds them into butter for a sauce. Finally, Mama makes a heavy porridge. We eat this every day, with pumpkin leaves or wild spinach or okra, and occasionally meat or fish soup. Sitting and eating with my family makes life feel almost normal again.

4

Because there are no classes, every student old enough to help rebuild the school joins in. Chieng, Majok and I remove wreckage and carry timber, which is split by the men. Others collect sisal and young palm tree leaves to be used as binding. Cement, boxes of nails, iron bars and iron sheeting have been brought into Pacong by truck. No more thatched roof for this new building. Like Waterman said, it's going to be better than the old one.

He's here with his sleeves pushed up, moving wheelbarrows of rubble like the rest of us. It's hard work but Waterman keeps us in good spirits. Everyone is doing what they can. I try not to think about Miss Ayen, and how she will never see the new school.

Some of us are better workers than others. After a few days, Chieng loses interest and sits himself down in a wheelbarrow. He convinces Majok to give him a ride, and they rush wildly around people and piles of debris.

I'm glad to see him play. Akol would have liked that. These days Chieng walks with his shoulders hunched forward, like he's carrying something heavy. And Thiko's eyes have the look of someone who's just woken from a nightmare. Even Majok is different. I've seen him standing and staring at birds as if he's never seen them before.

Every Sunday we go to church. I don't like going, although I do like the singing and drums and the way the girls dance with their eyes closed, swaying like palms in the wind, their faces serene, voices and hands lifted to heaven. You can feel God when they sing. But I don't like all the praying we do. It makes me sleepy, kneeling in silence with my eyes shut for so long. If I make the mistake of falling asleep, I get a bony elbow in the ribs from Grandpa.

Grandpa loves to pray and he always senses if I'm sleeping, even when he's deep in prayer. I think he keeps one eye cracked open to track me. He talks about God all the time, as if he's his best friend.

Sure enough, I do fall asleep and Grandpa elbows me. The minister is saying we must not surrender to the work of evil. We must stay strong and trust in the power of God, who will punish those who do evil. Life will go on, nothing can stop that. He tells us students to stay close together in this time of trouble, to be with each other as much as we can, until it's time to sleep.

So after church, Thiko, Chieng and Majok come home with me

and we sit outside around a fire and wait for Grandpa to come and tell us stories.

We all love listening to Grandpa's stories. He takes a stool on the other side of the fire, and with the breeze blowing the warmth of the flames over our skin he tells the tale of the tortoise that ran faster than the cheetah, and another about how the hyena became limp. We're happy to have something other than the bombing to think about.

When we have eaten and everyone has left, I lie in bed and look out at the stars. The night is quiet. I'm not sure how long I've been lying there when I hear something that sounds like gunfire.

At first I think it's my mind playing tricks, replaying the day of the bombing, but there it is again. It's definitely gunfire. It seems to be coming from the centre of the village, not very far away.

I jump up from my bed and find that Mama and Nyanbuot are up too. There's another burst of gunfire. Mama motions us to be quiet and peers cautiously out of the window.

I hold my breath. After a moment, I can't help myself and whisper, 'What can you see, Mama?'

'Nothing. It's too dark.'

'Shall I turn the flashlight on?' I fight to keep my voice from shaking. Next to me Nyanbuot quivers.

'No,' Mama says. 'We don't want to attract attention.'

'I'm scared of rats,' Nyanbuot whimpers.

'Those we can put up with,' Mama says. 'It's the two-legged rats we need to worry about.'

We stand there feeling helpless, and when there's been no further firing for a while Mama says, 'Let's go back to bed. Take deep breaths. Close your eyes. Pray to the Lord.'

To reassure Nyanbuot, I crawl under the bed she shares with Mama to check for rats, and also snakes. There are none for the moment, but that could change. Once, when I was working in the garden with Grandpa and came inside to get a hoe, I found a large snake in the hut, black and thick with a broad head. It flicked its tongue at me but otherwise remained still. I didn't know what kind of snake it was or how fast it might be, or how much poison it might have. I froze.

'Grandpa!' I shouted. 'Get your biggest spear and help me!'

He came to the door and looked in. 'You don't fight snakes with spears,' he said, and reappeared a moment later with a stick in his hand. He killed the snake with it. 'There, you're alright now.'

He put a hand on my shoulder to calm me and led me back outside. 'You see that tree there?' he said, pointing to the end of the garden. 'If a snake ever bites you, you must use its roots for medicine. Dig it up, crush it or pound it and squeeze the juice into your mouth. And remember, a spear for a lion, a stick for a snake.'

This scene lingers with me as I drift into sleep. When something brushes my leg I jerk awake, biting back a cry. I don't want to scare my sister. I can hear a rat scurrying across the floor. I pull both legs in tight to my body, curling up like a cat, and finally fall back asleep.

Then the sound of heavy footsteps reaches my ears. It might be a dream. But it might not be.

I swim up through sleep and the noise is real. More footsteps. I slip out from bed and crawl to the window. The rest of the family are asleep. The moon is up now and I peek out just far enough to see while remaining hidden. There's a man nearby. He's little more than a silhouette, but I can make out the beret he wears. There are other men a little further off. I step back from the window and press myself to the wall, squeezing my eyes shut.

Then suddenly the door of our hut rattles. My eyes fly open. Someone is throwing their weight against the door and I'm about to scream but Mama is beside me, putting her hand over my mouth and a finger to her lips. She pulls her hand away and hugs Nyanbuot, who has crept over to us. Thon slumbers on.

'Use the butt of your rifle,' a loud voice commands. The door holds firm.

Time has stopped but I'm aware of every excruciating second. Mama's hand grips mine. My throat is dry. God, please make them go, I pray silently, please make them go away.

And unbelievably they do. There's the sound of footsteps again, then silence folds over us once more.

But we remain huddled, too terrified to move. A dog barks somewhere in the village, followed by a woman's scream, and I know it's not just our door they're banging on. We stay quiet for a long time, fearful of making any noise.

Finally I open the shutter and peer out. 'I can see about twelve of them,' I whisper to Mama. 'They look like rebels. They're standing by the big mahogany tree on the path to Chieng's house. They all have guns.'

I worry that they will go to Chieng's hut but they turn away, down the hill, like they're just out taking a moonlight stroll.

'They're gone,' I say at last.

Mama is not convinced. 'They might be gone now,' she says, 'but this is far from over. We must pray.'

When morning comes I don't want to think about the night before. I want to scratch it from my mind, and I have the school rebuilding to help me. Waterman is there again to direct us. The women and girls from the village, including Momo, Mama and Thiko, bring food and water. We work hard, until gathering clouds send us home.

Thiko comes with me, and once the rain has stopped we go to find Chieng and Majok. She takes my hand and we run. The sticky heat of the air has lifted and the mud is smooth and warm between my toes.

We both love running. We run to school, run home, race in the fields where the goats graze, and whenever Thiko and I run, Majok and Chieng can never keep up. They follow us now, until we come to the shop near the school road. The building has holes all over it from being shot at.

Thiko lets go of my hand and crosses the road. 'Juba, come here,' she calls in a bubbly voice, the one she has when she's excited. 'That Oprah show is on the television again.'

Chieng and Majok look at me eagerly and the three of us rush over to the shop. The owner charges people to watch his television but we don't have money. One of the bullet holes gives a good view of the television, though, and Thiko is looking through it.

'She's talking to that girl Claire, from *Playing God*.'

'Her real name is Angelina Jolie,' I say. 'Claire is her name in the movie.'

'She's so beautiful,' says Thiko. 'I like her.'

Chieng is growing impatient. 'My turn,' he says, pushing forward. And soon Majok nudges him aside to take a look. He giggles at something funny, which makes us all want to watch together. I grab his shoulder and pull him away and then put my hands on the wall and peep through.

The people in the shop watching Oprah laugh when she and her audience laugh. I'm at the peephole for only moments, it seems, before Chieng says it's his turn again. I soak up the bright image for a few seconds longer then step aside. When Thiko taps him on the shoulder with her well-shaped fingers and clean nails he snaps, 'A minute.'

'Be fair, Chieng.' Thiko crosses her arms. I cannot think how she keeps her nails so clean.

'I am being fair. You be fair.'

'You've had a lot longer than I did,' I say.

'You would take her side, Juba.'

'What's that supposed to mean?'

'Come on, Chieng, move,' Majok says.

'In a minute!' Chieng is yelling now and it brings the shop owner bursting around the side of his shop with a stick.

'Pay or get out!' he yells. He doesn't wait for any offer of payment but is already swinging.

Chieng and Majok race away like cheetahs. Thiko grabs my arm and we set off after them, up the little hill behind the shop. The owner won't go too far from his shop while there are people inside. At the top of the slope we stand defiantly, waiting to see what he'll do.

He shakes his stick at us then stalks inside, leaving us giggling. But then he's back out with a bowl of water in his hands. He throws dirt into the bowl to make a paste and he smears this over our peephole.

So that's that. We go back to the school and start work. As I hand things up to the man doing the roof, I keep thinking how wonderful it would be to be wealthy and have my own TV. I could watch Oprah, movies, anything I wanted, right in my own home.

Once, Waterman paid for some of us to watch Oprah inside the shop. Afterwards I asked him who else watched Oprah and he said the whole world did. Everyone sitting in that shop today was watching and listening so intently that none of them moved or spoke. I think Oprah must be a very important person.

Next day, I discover that Thon has lost one of our goats, but instead of getting angry I pat him on the shoulder and say, 'It's okay, it's happened to the best of us.'

'I didn't mean to,' Thon says.

'You can look at it as a reminder to be more careful next time, and to pay attention. Don't let the goats be smarter than you.'

He lifts his chin. 'I am smarter than a goat!'

Thon is a funny boy and can be stubborn. A couple of months ago we were eating a chicken thigh. He ate his share and then demanded mine. When I refused he cried and ran to Mama.

'Juba ate all the chicken,' he said between sobs.

'Juba?'

I didn't answer, I just continued to eat my chicken.

'Juba!' Mama said more loudly. 'Bring your brother's chicken right now.'

'Mama, I took half and gave him half. He ate his share. Then he wanted mine.'

'You know to let your brother take the biggest part. You're older.'

'But if I did that, your wicked boy would have eaten the whole thigh.'

Mama slapped my leg then and sent me to fetch water.

But now I don't slap Thon, I tousle his hair. 'Never fear, Juba is here. I will find that missing goat.' I grab my stick and dash out the door.

My father used to tell us over and over that we must never lose a goat. He was a big man, tall and strong with sharp, bright eyes that made me think he could see for miles. His legs and arms reminded me of an ancient tree. The war took him. He died on his knees so his family could live.

The night it happened was dark. There was no moon and so no one stayed outside for stories, like we always did when the moon shone. But that didn't stop Deng and me telling each other stories in bed. I was telling one about a fox and a jackal when he put a finger to his lips to hush me. Deng is older than me, so he always bossed me around. My father told me I had to listen to him because Deng was the firstborn.

It was government soldiers who came that time. They ordered us all outside and told my father they knew he supported the rebels. They said that three days ago he had welcomed rebels with the meat of a whole goat, and other food.

My father kept saying that he didn't support either the rebels or the government soldiers, he was just a simple farmer. He explained that ten students had come to our hut that day. They were passing through the village and wanted to rest until the sun cooled down, then they would continue on to wherever they were going. My father had never met them before, and had only behaved as he would with any visitors. Visitors are respected in our culture. My father asked their names and chatted with them, and because he had killed a goat and was now roasting it, he shared it with them. After they'd eaten, the students left. Nobody had spoken about rebels, governments or the war.

The soldiers refused to believe this. One of them told my father to kneel, and when he didn't respond the man pointed his gun at the rest of us. I felt Mama's fingers squeeze me even tighter and my father immediately knelt. The soldier put his gun to my father's head and I looked away. Then came the gunshot.

The soldiers turned and walked calmly off into the dark night.

Mama howled and threw herself on my father's limp body, sobbing and praying to God to bring him back to life. I kept waiting for him to move, but he never did. Deng just stood there motionless. He wasn't crying. He was never the same after that night. None of us were.

Now, as I head off in search of the goat, smoke from cooking fires drifts on the morning breeze. There's no rain today and the ground is hard. No one is working in their garden. Women call to each other over their fences as they hang up laundry or sweep their yards. The tea-women are going to market dressed in rags and carrying straw baskets on their backs. Children shriek with laughter as they chase each other along the paths and dogs bark as they run after them. Men are off to the school to continue the reconstruction. The building is almost finished, and Grandpa says that when it's finally done a great white bull, a symbol of health, will be killed in celebration, because this new school will be more than bricks and timber and iron sheets, it will be a beacon of light in the darkness.

I come to where the road splits off like ribs and I take the path that leads into the forest. Yesterday Thon took the herd to the fields, but maybe the missing goat has wandered in among the trees. I follow a stream that leads to a waterfall. I can hear voices as I get closer and then I see that girls from the village are gathered at the pool. Thiko is with them. This is where they come to wash their clothes, and to swim.

Without thinking I duck behind a tree. I don't want to spy on the girls but I know they'll shout at me if I walk in on them. A few are already in the pool, others are at the water's edge, giggling as they undress. They splash in and swim to the end where the water is shallow and calm. The spray of the water catches the light and gleams.

Thiko is gathering her braided hair and tying it back out of the way, and then she starts washing her clothes. I can see her breasts. I've never seen her breasts before. They are small and firm and round like sweet fruit. I swallow hard. How many times have we played together? Too many to count.

I realise I've been holding my breath. As quietly as I can I retreat, and once I'm out of sight of the pool I straighten up and run. For a moment back there I forgot I was looking for a lost goat.

I jog along with the sun warm on the top of my head, feeling lighter and somehow more alive than I have in days. It's as though God is back in control, smiling down on me. He will not let anything bad happen to us again.

I call out for the goat as I push through the undergrowth, but there's no goat. I run for hours, still with no luck, and when my body starts to tire I slow my pace, resisting the desire to turn and head home. My lightness has gone and I worry that I will never find this goat.

A heavy feeling settles over me when I think this, and I pick up my pace again, as if I can outrun the feeling. I stub my big toe on a rock and a hot pain washes through me. I stop to check it and see that I've nearly ripped the toenail off. I keep moving, panting now from pain and a feeling of dread. It's my left foot that I've hurt again. The last time I stumbled it was on my left foot, and I got caught and whipped by a man whose garden had been destroyed by my goats. The left foot is bad luck. I hope that goat hasn't damaged someone else's garden. It's time to head home.

I'm not far from Pacong when I hear a loud crack, followed immediately by another, a hard, ugly sound that rings through my bones. It's a sound I've heard before. Please, no, I think, not again.

Maybe it's nothing. But when I reach the edge of the village there's a noise like a thunder roll, one loud clap after another. The sky is as clear as a plate of glass and there's not a drop of rain in sight. And so I know. They're back.

I scramble up a rise to see what's happening, squinting against the sun. A line of camouflaged jeeps, the sort used by government soldiers, pours from the bushes as though expelled by dark magic. Tanks follow. They swarm through the field to the village, spitting fire and throwing up dust. Soldiers jump from the jeeps and race through the huts. They're soldiers of the Sudanese government, shouting to each other in Arabic.

All I can think of is getting home to my family. I run so fast it feels as though my feet aren't touching the ground. I forget the pain in my toe but I can feel the blood pound in my ears with every step.

Near our house it is chaos. A blur of people screaming, crying and running in every direction. Homes are on fire.

'Mama!' I yell, willing my legs to move faster, even though the muscles burn and my lungs feel as if they're about to explode.

'Into the jungle!' I hear someone shout. 'That's our only chance!'

Should I turn around and run back out of the village with these people? The air is so thick with smoke I can't see our hut. Where are Mama and Grandpa and Momo, my little brother and sister? I don't know what to do. The flames leap from one thatched roof to the next, hideously bright. There's more smoke than oxygen in the air now.

'Get your spears!' I hear a villager yell and men run to grab them, but who could hope to fight a gun with a spear?

Two boys from my school bolt past me, straight across my path. Soldiers are shooting at random. I dive behind a tree, my eyes watering from the smoke. I hug my knees to my chest, telling myself I'm okay, I'm okay, I'm okay, trying to calm my breathing. The whole world seems to be spinning.

Timing my move I get to my feet, and staying low I follow the path towards home, my eyes straining to see familiar forms. Again I think of running away with the others but I must find my family first. They're fine, I repeat to myself over and over. I will find them and then we'll run together. All of us.

I reach Thiko's hut and my head reels when I see that it's engulfed in flames. Just then a new sound fills the air. It's the chants and shouts of the men of Pacong. Twenty warriors charge up, whooping and whistling battle cries, spears brandished. They rush at the soldiers.

I watch transfixed, wanting to believe that the warriors of my village can triumph, can put an end to this madness. One of them throws a spear and it hisses as it glides through the air, striking a soldier in the chest. The gun drops from his hand and he falls. His comrades barely glance at him, he is left there alone.

The minutes that follow are unbelievable, with spears dominating rifles, the warriors overpowering the soldiers, felling them like trees. But then a jeep rolls in, more soldiers spill out, firing their rifles before their feet even hit the ground. It's over in seconds.

I turn my head and vomit. I want to make it out of Pacong alive but I don't know how. God give me strength, I beg.

Somehow I manage to find our hut and it is not on fire. But men are still shouting, and screaming women are being dragged away by soldiers. I see two of them pulling on the same woman, like a pair of hyenas fighting over a goat. Another woman is screaming as her clothes are ripped off her. There's something familiar about her and I stop. It's Momo!

I drop to my knees and close my eyes for a second. But only a second. I know that if someone is to help Momo it will have to be me. Grandpa is nowhere in sight.

But as when the school was bombed, I can't move. My stomach is a knot of tangled snakes. Momo is screaming and scrabbling in the dirt. I must *do* something. Spying a stick not far off, I crawl over to grab it, wait until the soldier has his back to me, then I charge at him, brandishing my stick.

'No!' I scream. 'Leave her alone!' There's no room in me for fear now.

The soldier turns. An ugly smile forms on his face as he brings the butt of his rifle down on my shoulder. The pain causes my legs to collapse beneath me. I drop my stick and roll on the ground, unaware of anything but pain.

'Thinks he's a warrior, this one!' laughs the soldier. He flips me roughly over onto my back and looms above me, smiling his broken-toothed sneer. All I can do is let my eyes close and hope it will be over soon.

And then I hear my name being called and my eyes fly open in time to see Grandpa shove the soldier aside, flinging him into the dirt like he's a straw doll. Then my ageing grandfather is fighting the soldier with his fists, his feet, until the soldier pulls a knife from his belt and stabs Grandpa in the thigh.

'Grandpa!' I wail as blood soaks through his pants.

But the wound only seems to give him more strength. He knocks the knife out of the soldier's hand and punches him in the face. The man falls and Grandpa falls with him, striking repeatedly, until the soldier lies motionless. Grandpa stays atop him a moment, head bowed, chest heaving. Then he takes a deep breath and gets up, wiping his bloody knuckles on his clothes.

He checks to see that Momo is alright and then looks at me. How old he looks. He is ancient, as though thousands of years of sadness sit behind his eyes. But he has felled a man half his age. I can't believe it.

'Grandpa!' I fall on my knees before him. The dark stain on his thigh is spreading. I blink back the tears. 'Oh Grandpa.'

Around us the screaming and mayhem and burning continue, but he kisses my forehead and the familiar smell of his warm brown skin overwhelms me. I sob in huge, shuddering breaths.

'Juba,' he says, tipping my head up, 'open your eyes.'

I do. And I see the look in his eyes has changed.

'Juba, listen to me well,' Grandpa says. 'You must leave right now. No – do not argue with me. You must leave now. And do not turn back. No matter what you hear or see, you must keep going. Run as fast as you can. Go immediately.'

'But what about —'

'*Now!* You're a good runner. Use that talent, you will need it. Run as fast as you can away from the village. Take the road over the hills. There'll be others fleeing. Find them and go with them. They will lead you to a place for refugees.'

I bite my lip and nod mutely.

'Do you hear me?' he says, giving me a shake, the way he does when I've been disobedient. The pain flares in my shoulder. 'You must *run*. Your mother and brother and sister were at the well. God alone knows their fate.'

'But I can fight!' I plead. I don't want to leave him and Momo here. He's badly injured. 'This is my village. I can fight, Grandpa!'

'No you can't, Juba. Do not confuse bravery with wisdom. You're going to have to fight one day, but not now in Pacong. You're going to run. You're going to survive. Not by using your fists, but your heart and mind.'

'But I don't want to leave,' I sob. 'I want to stay with you and Momo.'

As more shots ring out, Grandpa struggles to his feet and pulls me up after him, and he literally shoves me away. 'I'm not asking you to go,' he says. 'I'm ordering. *Go!*'

Two more soldiers have settled on Momo like carrion. Grandpa grabs the dead soldier's knife and limps as fast as he can towards them while I stand swaying with dizziness. He manages to stab one soldier in the neck, and the other rolls off Momo, yanking up his pants, trying to retrieve his rifle.

'Run *now*, Juba!' Grandpa yells without turning around. 'God will lead you! He will protect you!'

But Momo is lying there unmoving, and I can see blood seeping from beneath her, turning the dust into dark red mud. This cannot be real. It cannot.

Grandpa, with a mighty grunt, plunges the knife into the soldier's stomach, but the soldier has already reached his gun and at the exact same moment he brings it up and fires. The two fall apart from each other, both gasping for breath.

I scramble over to Grandpa as the blood bubbles from his mouth. He's trying to speak but no sound comes out. The hole in his chest is smoking. His eyes already have a faraway look.

'Grandpa, no, don't go! *Please* don't leave me . . .' I touch his face and suddenly I know he is right. 'Okay,' I say, my mouth close to his ear. 'I will do as you say. I will run and I won't look back. I'm going, Grandpa.'

His face seems almost contented. I know my words have reached him. His head lolls to one side, his cheek kissing the dust, like he's merging into the soil beneath him.

The wind holds still and silent while the violence rages around us. I am drowning and there is no hope of being saved. My heart is raw. I have no ribs, no skin. But somehow I can still feel the oxygen flooding into my lungs.

I stand up and run.

5

Dead bodies litter the village. I come to the fork in the road and see something familiar. My goats. Soldiers are leading them away. For a moment I want to charge at them but then I remember my promise to Grandpa. I bend over while I run, like I do when I want to surprise a gazelle during a hunt.

I clear the eastern edge of the village and reach the jungle. Its deep green shadows welcome me. I must not let myself think of Grandpa and Momo, but other thoughts are swirling in my head. Where is Mama? What if she's back in the village somewhere with Nyanbuot and Thon, waiting for me to come home? Or out looking for me? Breathing in the smoke while I'm running in the opposite direction?

Or maybe they've managed to flee, and are safely waiting for me somewhere ahead.

The idea that I might be running towards them spurs me on, although my shoulder and head throb and my lungs burn. I leap over branches that try to grab at me. They will not hold me back. And government soldiers will not kill me, because I am strong. I am a potential freedom fighter.

In this crazy state I nearly run into a tank. I shin up a tree just in time, praying I haven't been seen. There's no way I can run now, the tank is too close. The weight of it makes the tree vibrate. I press my face into the trunk and close my eyes. I don't want to see it coming at me. Twigs snap on the ground below as it rumbles past, without hitting my tree.

It pushes on towards the village and I make my way down. At the last branch I let go and jump to the ground. As I do, my shorts snag on the branch and are all but ripped off me. I reach the ground to find half of them still in the tree. The half left hanging on me is useless, so I rip it off altogether and throw it into the bushes and start running again in just my shirt.

I hate this running. It's not like racing with my friends. I hope they're safe. I haven't seen anyone from the village since I set off.

A new sound makes me look up. Helicopters. Two of them, hovering like giant locusts. I've never seen a helicopter this close before. Their terrifying blades slice the air in a metallic blur. I keep going.

I lose track of the time. Deeper in the jungle everything is silent. After the chaos and noise of the village, the quiet is disconcerting. The trees are still, the grass doesn't move. The only sound comes from inside my head, where my brain beats like a ticking clock, loud and insistent.

Then a breeze moves around me, stirring the leaves and grass. It seems to carry a murmur and I turn, but no one is there. The treetops shiver. The hairs on the back of my neck are standing on end. All at once explosions are happening again and the silence is over. I glimpse rocket launchers mounted on truck beds as I race on. Trees ignite. Branches, dirt and debris fall from the sky. The force of an explosion nearby knocks me to the ground and I huddle there, hands covering my head, splintered wood pelting my body. When I look up I can see a raw crater in the earth. A tree has been completely split in half. The air is thick with dust and the angry whistling of bombs. From somewhere comes screaming.

Then, as suddenly as they started, the bombs stop. I am unhurt.

I sit up and look around. Now there are soldiers on the run. I get up and run again myself. I try to imagine myself in a man's body so that I take bigger strides. Better yet, I'm so huge I can crush the soldiers and grind them up like bugs. Dust is still boiling around me and up ahead there's a fresh jeep full of soldiers. I can make out two men from my village on its bed, bound hand and foot. I drop behind cover, my throat constricting, but the soldiers are hunting other prey. A woman about Mama's age, with a child. The soldiers take aim and shoot her down and without thinking I scream.

They whip around. Fool! Why didn't I keep quiet? I dart out and sprint. The cracking of gunfire follows me. Tiny clouds spurt up at my feet. I pretend I'm hunting, with Thon-gool loping along at my side, tongue lolling joyfully out of his mouth. We are chasing a gazelle, swift and determined. A gazelle does not stop running until you kill it, or your dog grabs hold of its legs and brings it crashing to the ground. I will run like that gazelle but I will not be killed. I will find Mama, Nyanbuot and Thon. I will find Thiko and Chieng and Majok. I will tell them how I outran the soldiers.

I run like mad. When I trip and fall again I get up and keep going. Gunshots echo behind me. But if you can hear a gun, you're not dead. I race along a trail covered in dead leaves that takes me to where the trees are taller. Every muscle in my body is screaming at me to stop but I force myself on. Twigs dig into my heels, stones lacerate the soles of my bare feet. I leap over logs and push my way through hanging vines and low branches.

I don't know how far I've run when I realise I haven't heard a shot in a while. Or shouting. I slacken my pace, but it's hard to slow down even though my body wants nothing more. When I do drop to half speed, my knees give way. For a long time I kneel under the canopy, chest heaving, trying to get my breath.

I can hear crickets. Their sound takes me back to times when Thiko and I would run through the tall grass to the river's edge, where the cold mud enveloped our toes, the water flowed around our legs, and my hand grasped hers. And I wonder if I will ever be that happy again.

When my breathing has calmed I move again. Countless feet have formed this trail that I follow, have bent the browned grass to one direction. My people will be out here. It won't be long before I find them. I trot along as the sun is starting to sink behind trees and it makes the smoke hanging in the air look like blood. I need to think about finding somewhere to sleep, or at least spend the night. My rumbling stomach probably won't let me sleep. I haven't eaten anything since setting off to look for my goat. It would be safest to climb a tree, one with a wide fork in its branches, but I'm not sure I have the energy for that.

I'm still trying to decide what to do when I hear a crashing through the undergrowth. My ears strain but I can't hear any voices. My muscles are tensed and I'm ready to leap when a warthog charges out. I gulp fresh air into my lungs as I watch it run off. I'm not afraid of a warthog, no boy can be afraid of a warthog. But I know it's afraid of me because its meat is very tasty.

I've barely recovered from that encounter when there's a fresh disturbance on the other side of the path. I can't tell if it's an animal or a human and before I can move, the bushes part and out rushes Waterman.

His face is streaked with dirt and dried blood. His clothes are in shreds. I blink in shock at seeing him alive, at seeing anyone I know alive. His eyes, when he sees me, look just as shocked.

Then his face relaxes and a huge smile spreads across it. 'Juba!'

For a second I think he will come over and hug me. But he just stands next to me, looking down at me, his smile growing even wider. 'Boy, am I glad to see you,' he says. 'Are you alright? Are you hurt?'

My shock gives way to instant joy. 'You're the first person I've met since I started running!' I say. 'I'm okay but . . .' I can't bring myself to tell him about Grandpa and Momo. I still can't believe they're really gone.

'I had to dodge some soldiers earlier,' Waterman says. 'So you're not the first person I've seen, but you're the first person I'm glad to see.' And he laughs heartily, even though he hasn't said anything funny. The sound of his laughter is nearly as good as food.

'Where are you going?' I ask. 'I know there's a refugee place but I don't really know where or how far.'

'Just getting away from the soldiers is good for now,' he says. 'We'll figure out the rest later. It's nearly dark.'

'It is,' I nod. 'We should find a tree. That's the safest bet.' My energy has revived on meeting Waterman, at no longer being alone.

'Sounds wise.' He looks around. 'I think I'll let you decide. All these trees look the same to me.'

We set off and I say, 'Waterman, did you see my family before you left Pacong? Or Thiko or Chieng and Majok? What about the other kids from school?'

'I'm sorry, Juba,' he says, 'I didn't see your family or friends. I did see some of the students but they were . . .' He draws his mouth into a tight line and doesn't finish his sentence.

'Where were you when the soldiers came?'

'On my way to the school. At first I thought I was the target and then I realised it was the whole of Pacong. I'll spare you the details but I got away, though without my car. Or my satellite phone, which would be good to have right now. We could have gotten some help, but instead the organisation I work for will have no idea where I am.'

Waterman keeps swatting at his face. 'If the soldiers don't get me, these bugs will do me in,' he says. In the dim light I can see the welts on his delicate white skin. He won't be used to walking through this land at night.

Before full darkness descends, I find a tree that seems to rise up forever, its canopy a distant cloud of green. Its thick branches will provide protection.

Waterman eyes it warily. 'I'm supposed to be able to sleep here? Not sure how that's going to happen.'

But we both manage to climb it and I find a good spot among the branches. 'Here,' I say, 'prop yourself in there and lean against the trunk. You won't fall out.'

He gives me another sceptical look but does as I say. 'Ah,' he says, settling in. 'Not so bad.'

I find a spot of my own. When I used to go on hunts with my father and Grandpa, sometimes for a week at a time, we'd sleep in trees. Once, walking at night, Grandpa and I surprised a lion. I stopped dead in my tracks and Grandpa bumped into me, nudging me forward. The lion must have thought I was coming for him, because he pounded the ground with his tail, stirring up dust. Grandpa pulled me behind him, then knelt and began singing one of his warrior songs.

'Don't scream,' he told me. I wondered how this would be possible, with a lion about to attack. My knees shook. 'Stay very still,' he warned.

He raised his spear and the lion charged. I screamed and squeezed my eyes shut. Over my screams I heard a thud, and then Grandpa singing his song once more.

I opened my eyes. The lion lay on the ground.

'Cut off the tail,' Grandpa told me.

I drew my knife, stepped around him and grabbed the lion's tail. It twitched. I almost screamed again as I jumped back.

Grandpa laughed. 'Juba, how can you be a warrior if you fear a dead lion?'

But the animal was still alive. Its ribcage heaved up and down, even with Grandpa's spear lodged in its chest. I knelt down and cut off the tail, feeling sick. It flicked again before I cut it.

When I told this story to the boys in my village, they didn't believe me. They didn't think I could be that brave. And now, sitting here in this tree, I can't believe that Grandpa is dead. I can't believe I'll never see him again. I didn't know, that day he killed the lion, how many worse things there were to be afraid of.

Above us the sky is a deep black pinpricked with stars. Below me Waterman shifts.

'Everything okay?' I ask.

'This tree is actually far more comfortable than I ever would have thought,' he says. 'Either that or I'm so exhausted it could be a bed of nails and it'd still feel like a featherbed.'

'Do people really sleep in beds made of feathers?' I ask.

'Some people, I guess,' he laughs.

I try to imagine plucking enough chicken feathers to make a mattress.

'I had a feather-filled quilt at home,' Waterman says. 'The feathers poked out of it sometimes and they scratched. Plus it got too hot. I never liked having too many covers on. Hey, at least I don't have to worry about that tonight.'

Waterman sighs, but not in a sad way. 'You know,' he says, 'however bad things get, looking up at the sky always puts it in perspective. Juba, do you ever look at it and think how tiny you are?'

'All the time,' I say, just as a star falls. I wish hard for the safety of my family and friends. Then I think back to just after the school bombing and how I wanted to ask Waterman why he was in our village, why he wanted to help us. Now I don't think he'll take offence at the question.

'Waterman,' I say.

'Nathan,' he says. 'My first name is Nathan. You can call me that.'

'Okay. Nathan, there's something I've been wondering about. Why are you here?'

He laughs. 'Why am I up in this tree with you right now? Or why am I here in general? Like, what did God put me on this earth for?'

'No, I mean why are you here in Sudan? Why do you want to help us so much? You look like the sort of person who could be doing anything at all. You could be in America still. You could be safe. You could live in a big house. And then you wouldn't have to be up this tree with me.'

'No, I suppose I wouldn't,' he says, and then he's silent for a while. 'I did grow up in a big house, in fact. And my parents bought us pretty much anything we wanted, my brother and me. We had expensive cars, all that. My father was a banker and it was just assumed that once we graduated we'd go to work in his bank. I know it must sound crazy to you, Juba, but I didn't want the kind of life my parents had.'

He's right, it does sound crazy. I can't begin to imagine what that kind of childhood must be like. To have everything you want, to have a job just waiting for you. To drive in expensive cars. Why would anyone want to leave that?

'You didn't want to work at a bank?' I ask. There are no banks in Pacong. I've never even seen a bank, but we read about them in school. 'Is working there so bad? It's not like looking after goats.'

'True. But that sort of life just isn't for me. I never wanted a job where the hardest thing my hands have to do all day is moving stuff around on a desk.'

'But it's safe in America, isn't it? Don't you want to be safe?'

'Well, yes . . .' he says slowly. 'And that's another luxury I had growing up, the luxury of being safe. But I also knew there are plenty of people in the world who don't know what it means to be safe, and I wanted do something more useful with my life. Sad to say, this is impossible for some people to understand, my father being one of them.'

Nathan shifts a little to look up in my direction. 'You really want to hear about this?' he asks. 'After everything that happened today?'

I do. I want the distraction of his story. I'm tired and I'm hungry but I'm scared that if I sleep it will bring nightmares. 'Yes,' I say. 'Tell me about your life in America. I want to know.'

'Okay, well, my older brother did everything expected of him when he graduated college, but I went travelling in Third World countries, and after a while my father told me I had a choice. I could continue living the life of a hobo, as he put it, or I could do the right thing and go to work at the bank. Settle down, get married, have kids. Basically live the exact same life he had. If I didn't do this I would be pretty much disowned.'

He coughs a little and he sounds nervous. Or embarrassed maybe. 'Juba, I do know this must be hard for you to understand, given how poor your village is. Anyway, that was about the last conversation I ever had with my father. The thing about people like him is that their universe is very small. My father didn't interact with people who didn't look like him, talk like him, or have money like he did. Which is why I like to look up at the sky, especially at night. It reminds me how big the universe is.'

'Did you really never talk to your father again?'

'I never did. He died a year after we had that conversation. Car accident.'

Nathan is quiet again for a while and then says, 'Who knows, we might've been able to patch things up at some point, but people can get very set in their thinking.'

His story is amazing. He has left behind such a comfortable, easy life and I'm still not entirely sure why. It's hard to think that anyone would choose life in Pacong over a life like that. Maybe if there wasn't a war . . .

'Do you ever wish you'd done what your father wanted?' I ask him.

'No,' he says immediately. 'My brother has asked me the same thing, but I've never regretted my choice. Sure, I wouldn't be up here in this tree right now, but I also think I might never have felt truly alive. You know, we're actually no different, you and I. People are people at the end of the day. Even those soldiers out there – if they stopped to think about it for even a minute, they might realise it. We all live, eat and breathe on this same earth.'

I'm glad that despite everything that's happened he doesn't regret coming here. 'If more people thought like you did,' I say, 'things might be different in Pacong.'

'Everything always changes,' he says. 'That's the one guarantee there is in life, that nothing will stay the same.' He reminds me of Grandpa when he says that. 'And Juba, if I were to die in this tree tonight, I'd die a happy man, because I've lived the way I want to. I didn't let anyone tell me otherwise. And what I really want for you, and everyone else in Pacong, is to be able to say the same thing.'

Wow. This is a big thought.

'I'm not sure what that would even mean,' I say. 'What if I wanted to travel? How would I do it? I couldn't just get on a plane and go to another country.'

'I know there's no way you can do that, not now anyway. But still, sometimes the way finds you. If you want something hard enough.'

'Do you really think that?' I can't tell if he's just trying to give me hope.

'Yes, I really do. People who want to control others are trying to fill the void in their own lives. But nothing's ever enough for those people. They take and take and take and run down whoever gets in their way. Sometimes, like today, they destroy them. Of course you can't just want something to happen and it immediately does, and you can't stop people behaving the way they do, but you can work toward making things happen for yourself. Especially you, Juba. You're bright, you're smart. You can do great things. Don't underestimate yourself.'

Nathan yawns. 'We should get some sleep now,' he says.

I close my eyes but sleep won't come. The night is full of growls and yips. The branches of a nearby tree are slapping each other in the wind. Baboons howl and bark. Maybe leopards are hunting them.

I open my eyes and stare into the dark. I imagine that my family is out there, safe, thinking of me. My ears have grown numb in the cold air and I rub them to warm them. A loud gurgle comes from my insides, and to stop myself feeling hungry

I pretend I'm hunting, that Grandpa is right here with Nathan and me. Tonight we are sleeping in this tree but tomorrow the three of us will get up together and we will hunt. We will kill. We three will eat.

I must have drifted off because next thing I know it's morning. The sunlight is a soft buttery yellow and mist is receding over the hills. The air is still cold but it's full of birdsong. I stretch, then look down to see that Nathan is already on the ground.

I make my way down. 'Good morning, Nathan. How did you sleep?'

'I didn't fall out. And I climbed down on my own accord.'

I can tell how proud he is of this by the look on his face.

'It's a great morning, right?' He looks around and breathes deeply. 'You might think I'm nuts, Juba, because I'm sore and covered in insect bites, my clothes are filthy, and I've just escaped a massacre, but I still think there's more beauty in the world than ugliness.'

As if to challenge his statement, a lion roars in the distance. 'We should start walking,' I say.

We head back over to the path, where the grass has been trod by many feet. I feel certain we'll come across someone from the village today.

I am very glad to have Nathan's company. I talk to him about my family, about my father, about Deng and Nyanbuot and Thon. And I tell him what happened to Grandpa and Momo.

Nathan stops walking when I finish that story, and when he sets off again he doesn't speak for a long time.

At last he says, 'Juba, I'm so sorry. Your grandfather was such a fine man. So wise. I had the pleasure of talking with him several times through an interpreter, and hearing his stories. But Juba, you will keep him alive. You will be the storyteller now.'

Through my sadness I'm proud to think of Grandpa talking with Nathan, impressing him with his stories. And I know Nathan is right. Grandpa does live on through me.

We continue, winding in and out of hanging vines, pushing through foliage. The forest is full of creatures making all sorts of sounds. I tell Nathan about a vine that holds water, which you can drink when you're thirsty. Grandpa showed it to me when we went hunting, but it doesn't grow everywhere.

And as if to remind me further of Grandpa, a lion steps out onto the path ahead of us.

It's a male, with a raggedy mane, and it's thin. It doesn't look very healthy, which makes it dangerous. Lions usually only attack people when they're hungry, and this one looks like it hasn't eaten in a while. It stands there staring at us, tail lashing back and forth.

'Juba,' Nathan says in a low, terrified voice, not taking his eyes from it. 'I think we're going to have to part ways now. We need to run. I know you're a fast runner.'

But my feet feel like they're struck to the ground and I don't think I'll be able to move. It's just like when Grandpa told me to run from the village. I try to think what to do. The nearest tree has smooth bark and no branches until halfway up. I could climb it before the lion got to me but I don't think Nathan could.

The lion is standing and staring. Its paws look gigantic.

'You go in one direction, Juba, and I'll go in the opposite and maybe that will confuse it. When I give the word, we'll both run at once. Okay?'

The lion's mouth is open now, its huge jagged teeth are on display. In panic I grab a rock and throw it. It misses and the lion rushes forward and Nathan I both take off.

I can't tell where Nathan is headed but I haven't gone far before I hear strange noises behind me. Terrible noises. I don't let myself look back. I tell my ears not to listen and I force myself onward. I can't let myself think about the lion coming after me. I can't let myself think about it maybe getting Nathan. If I push my body as hard as it will go I can stop my thoughts from overwhelming me. I must not think about anything, I must just keep running as hard as I possibly can.

I don't know how long I run for but it feels like forever. I run until I'm so exhausted I can't lift my feet off the ground and I collapse.

I lie there with the wind knocked out of me, unable to draw breath. My whole body is rigid. My lungs are on fire. I keep trying to breathe but it seems that after all I've been through, I will end up dying here. But at last I'm able to take in a breath, then another, and my body starts to relax.

Only now do I realise I'm lying in a pile of fresh dung. I sit up. Every part of me aches.

Nathan, I think, where are you? He could be anywhere by now, that is if he's still alive. Those strange, terrible noises come back into my ears and I know in my heart what they mean.

I cry for Nathan. Such a good man, even kinder than I thought. I cry for him and for Grandpa and Momo, and for all the other innocent people who have been killed for no reason. I cry because

I've never felt this alone and because I don't know what to do. I can't remember ever feeling this scared. If I die out here, then Mama, Nyanbuot, Thon, Thiko and my other friends will be left not knowing what happened to me. Just like we don't know what happened to Deng.

It takes a long time for my tears to subside and my breathing to return to normal. I look up at the sky and I think of what Nathan said. The universe is big and everything in it wants to survive. I want to survive. So I can't lose hope. For Nathan's sake now, as well as Grandpa's.

I force myself to get up. I will keep walking. I'll follow the trampled paths like Grandpa told me to. But my shirt has been just about ripped in two now and I can't manage to tie it onto myself. It was too small for me anyway and is covered in dung. I yank it off and continue on naked.

There are voices in my head as I walk. There's Grandpa's voice telling me to follow the foot trails, to live. There's Mama's voice pleading with me to find her. And there's my own voice saying I could just stop, lie down and be done. There'll be no more pain. No bad memories.

I shake my head to rid myself of this voice and push on, alternating between walking and a running limp as the sun climbs higher. When the path nears the Nile, I step to the edge and cup my hands and drink. But I have no luck looking for food. I go back to the path and press on, passing a heap of large dry bones. Judging by their size, they must be an elephant's, or a rhino's.

When my shadow is taller than me I stop. It seems that another day will end without me encountering anyone from my village, and this thought makes me furious. My mind feels like a thousand flies are buzzing inside it. I kick a stone, punch a tree, and this calms me somehow.

I remind myself of my promise to Grandpa. I will rest and tomorrow I will keep walking. If I grow too weak to run or walk I will crawl. Even if vultures hover overhead, waiting for me to drop, I will not give up. I will not surrender myself to death. It will take me in time, but I will not give up easily. Death and I are head to head right now. But I cannot let it win. If I do, then Grandpa and Momo and Nathan will have died for nothing.

6

I'm searching for a tree to spend the night in when I hear voices. Outside my head this time, further along the path. My first thought is soldiers but these voices aren't Arabic, these people are speaking Dinka. They must be from Pacong!

I creep forward quietly in the dusk, not wanting to reveal myself yet, just in case. And then I'm blessed with a miracle. There are four figures up ahead and when one of them turns I see that it is Thiko.

No, I think, it can't be. I'm imagining it. It's a trick of my mind. But the boys with her sound familiar as well.

'Thiko?' I call, stepping into the open. My voice is croaky.

All four of them jump, their expressions changing from terror to shock and then instant joy. Thiko and Chieng shout, *'Juba!'* in unison and come running.

Thiko gives me a long hug and I squeeze her tightly. I never want to let her go. She smells of the sun. The warmth of her arms around my back lightens my heart, says everything is alright, everything is going to be okay. A lump forms in my throat but I won't let myself cry.

'I thought I'd never see you again,' she says when we pull apart.

Chieng and I grasp our right hands as we slap our shoulders with our left. I grimace when he does this, it revives the pain of the soldier's rifle butt. 'Good to see you,' he says, grinning madly.

'Good to see *you*.' Then, when we've let go, I ask, 'Have you seen my family?' I look from him to Thiko. They both shake their heads.

The two little boys with them are gazing up at me with wide eyes. They are Koko and Bagic, and their mother is a good friend of Chieng's mother. I tousle Koko's hair and rub Bagic on the shoulder.

'I can't believe what's happened,' I say to Chieng. 'I just . . .' I don't know how to say what I'm feeling.

'Me either,' he says. 'I was going to the bush, to the toilet, when I heard the *bang-bang tarraa-tarraa*. I just ran.'

Despite everything, I can't keep a crazy image from my mind. 'So, there was no more toilet?'

'No!' he says. 'I don't know what happened to it but I haven't felt like going since!'

We all laugh and it feels good to laugh.

'What about your family, Chieng?'

His face drops, all laughter gone. 'I didn't even think of trying to get back home. There was no time. People were running everywhere, so I'm hoping my family ran too.' He looks at me. 'And I don't know what happened to Majok.'

So here we are. Four boys and a girl without a home and without parents. Thiko hasn't seen her mother or sisters either.

'I was on my way home from the waterfall,' she tells me, and I notice that she still has the little green backpack she'd carried her washing in. 'The girls I was with ran straight off but I wanted to find my mother. Halfway to the village the gunfire and the screaming were too much. I got confused. I didn't know what to do. I turned back again and kept running.' She looks for a moment like she wants to cry.

It seems a lifetime ago that I came across the girls at the waterfall. 'How did you meet up with Koko and Bagic?' I ask.

Chieng tells me he was escaping the village with five others, including the two boys, when they saw soldiers up ahead. In the panic to flee they were separated. Chieng ran into the bushes to hide, covering his ears to block out the gunfire. He was too scared to move for a long time, but when he finally crept back towards the path, he found Bagic and Koko lying in a burrow, shaking and sobbing. Back on the path, the three of them continued on, and some hours later they came across Thiko sitting on anthill and struggling to pull a thorn out of her foot.

'That was a good moment!' says Thiko.

Chieng says, 'We think there's another group ahead of us but we haven't caught up yet. Maybe our families are with them. Or at least someone who might have seen them.' He bites his lip.

Thiko pats me on the arm and takes my hand. 'I can't believe it's really you,' she says. 'But I'm *so* glad it is.' She looks me up and down and then puts her pack on the ground and takes out a skirt. 'Here, put this on,' she says, holding it out to me.

I gape at her. 'Why would I wear a skirt?' Then I go suddenly red. I've completely forgotten that I'm naked. I grab the skirt and cover myself with it.

Thiko grins. 'I bet you'd rather be wearing a skirt than nothing if we come across a swarm of bees.'

I try not to groan. 'I can't believe you're bringing that up,' I say, turning my back to her to pull on the skirt and remembering the night a couple of years ago when Chieng and I went to the forest to collect honey. I wasn't wearing any pants because the only pair I had were torn and I'd left them with Grandpa to mend. The bees attacked and I got stung right on the penis. It swelled up to the size of a baby's arm and for the next few days I had to be careful how I walked. Chieng told everyone of course, and the girls couldn't stop giggling whenever I passed.

Now Chieng is laughing at me in the skirt. Koko and Bagic too. And that's enough to make me want to wear it. Their laughter is worth everything. Soldiers have destroyed our village and are hunting us down but we can still laugh.

'Thank you,' I say to Thiko, wanting to hug her again.

She smiles. 'It looks better on you than it does on me!'

My stomach growls, my hunger reawakened. 'Any food around?' I ask.

'Not that we've found so far,' Chieng says.

It's too late to search for food now, so we look for somewhere to spend the night. I don't say anything about Nathan, I don't want to scare them anymore than they've already been. And my own fear has subsided a little, if not the sadness. I am with my friends and regardless of what happens now, at least we're together. We will watch out for each other.

We suck on wild seeds to trick our minds into thinking we're eating. We cannot trick our bellies, though, and they all groan in discontented unison.

We walk only a little further before we come to a clearing, where we decide to stop. We gather wood for a fire and dry elephant grass for our beds. I'm not very good at starting a fire, so Chieng does it. He makes a small hole in a piece of kindling and places it on dry grass, then he puts a firestick between his palms and rubs it in the hole, twirling it harder and faster until a wisp of smoke appears. He continues until the grass catches alight. Thiko puts more grass around the flames and blows gently until they become strong and crawl at the wood.

Staring into the flames makes me think of home. The fire keeps growing but I can't stop shivering. Thiko scoots closer and wraps her arms around me, and that somehow feels much warmer than our little fire. An owl hoots nearby. Koko and Bagic, already nearly asleep, sit up startled.

'It's just an owl,' Chieng says gently. 'Go to sleep now.'

The moon is bright. I lie on my back and stare up at it for a long time before at last I sleep.

I wake before sunrise, cold, with only embers remaining of our fire. At first light we resume our trek. When a lion roars in the distance, I can hear little animals scurrying for their hideouts, though I can't see them. I pray that the lion won't cross our path.

A wind has sprung up and the air feels tense. We keep following the trail, scanning everywhere for something, anything, to eat.

'There!' Thiko exclaims, pointing to the top of a tree. 'Fruit!'

'What kind is it?' Chieng asks uncertainly. 'A lot of things aren't safe to eat out here.'

'I think it's okay,' Thiko says, peering upwards.

'But are you sure?'

'Well, not a hundred percent.'

Chieng shakes his head. 'Then we shouldn't eat it.'

Thiko looks at him, her chin raised. 'Would it be better if we starved? Because that's what's going to happen. These two,' she nods at Koko and Bagic, 'need to eat.' She turns to me. 'What do you think, Juba?'

Chieng is looking at me too. It seems I'm the tiebreaker.

'Well . . .' It's true that I don't know what kind of tree it is, and the fruit could be poisonous, but Thiko is right. Our options aren't too good right now.

Then I notice a couple of birds eating the fruit. 'Look,' I say, pointing. 'Grandpa told me once that most of the things that birds eat, people can eat too.'

'Okay,' Chieng says after a moment. 'Let's go.'

He and I climb the tree. It's a lot harder to do this in a skirt. Near the top I reach out to grab a piece of fruit and overbalance. I lose my grip on the branch, grab at another but it breaks and I plummet to the ground. Pain shoots through my leg.

'Don't move!' Thiko shouts, running over.

'Juba, are you okay?' Chieng calls down.

Thiko is kneeling beside me. 'Are you hurt?'

'My leg,' I moan.

'Let me see it.'

'No, don't touch it. What's wrong with it?'

She gives me a patient look. 'How am I going to tell you what's wrong with it if you won't let me touch it? I'll be as gentle as I can, I promise.'

'Fine then.' I grit my teeth. Her fingers are warm on my skin. She presses here and there. I grit my teeth harder.

'It's not broken,' she says finally. 'Here, let me help you up.' She gets me into a sitting position, and already the pain is receding.

Above us, Chieng begins tossing down fruit and Thiko holds out the bottom of her blouse to catch it. When Chieng is back on the ground we all feast. The fruit has a pale, bitter flesh but it's juicy and we gulp it down. In our hunger it tastes better than all the soup and sweet potato and fried chicken in the world. We eat until we can eat no more, then set off once more.

As the sky continues to brighten we can see another clearing up ahead, smaller this time. A warthog darts out from a bush, startling Bagic. He lets out a yell and we all laugh at him.

He grows defensive. 'Well, it could've been something scary!'

'Ah yes,' Chieng says, 'the ferocious man-eating warthogs.'

That's when I see it. Just beyond the clearing. A lion. It's sniffing the wind.

'Guys,' I say. None of them are looking, and Chieng is still too busy giving Bagic a hard time. 'Guys, *look*!'

Chieng turns around and his smile dies. The lion lifts its head and twitches its ears. It's another young male, and it too looks raggedy. Is it the same one that got Nathan?

As if it smells something tasty it comes towards us.

'Oh . . .' Bagic whimpers. 'It's going to eat us.'

'I'm not a good climber,' Koko says, his voice shaking.

'What should we do?' Chieng's eyes are wide in fear and he sounds panicky.

'Calm down!' Thiko hisses. 'You'll scare the boys.'

'They should be scared! There's a lion coming towards us, in case you hadn't noticed. We should *all* be scared!'

The animal has paused now, still some way from us. Thiko crosses her arms. 'Well, I'm not scared. Lions hardly ever attack people.'

'But sometimes they do,' I say. 'That's how Nathan died.'

It comes out before I can stop myself, and the four of them stare at me.

'Who's Nathan?' Chieng asks.

'Waterman,' I reply.

'What?' Thiko says. 'Did you say Waterman?'

'A lion ate Waterman?' Koko asks.

The shock on their faces is so strong I instantly regret telling them. It's as if, just as we thought at first he might not be real, we also thought nothing could hurt him. He was the one who left his country to come and help us, who told the mothers in the village how to keep their children healthy, who was determined to ensure a good education for us. It did not seem that he would ever share our fate. And now he has. He was just like one of us, just like he said.

'Yes,' I say, because there's no point lying.

'That's so terrible.' Thiko's eyes drop.

I'm keeping a careful watch on the lion but it hasn't moved any closer.

'It might've been sick,' I say to the two little boys. 'The other lion. That's maybe why it attacked. And there were only the two of us. A lion will be less likely to attack if there're five of us.'

But I can tell we're all thinking the same thing. That if a lion killed Waterman, it can kill any of us. I'm about to say something more when Thiko beats me to it.

'Okay,' she says. 'We need to scare it off. We need to shout. As loud as we can and all at once. And wave our arms. Be as big as we can be.' She looks at Koko and Bagic. 'Can you try to do that? Scream and yell, jump up and down, sound as fierce and as scary as you possibly can. Ready?'

We do it. We scream. Shout. Wave our arms. We jump up and down. Parrots burst from the trees. The lion doesn't move.

'It's not working,' Thiko says, and I can hear fear in her voice now.

'Run!' I yell, and we bolt, scattering like chickens at first and then joining up instinctively and making for the trees beyond the clearing.

There's a particularly tall tree ahead, with branches that look easy to climb. Koko might not be the best climber but he and Bagic are both fast. It's Thiko who's fallen behind for some reason. I turn to see she's limping slightly.

I remember the sounds I heard when I ran from the last lion. Thiko will not make those sounds, I will not allow it. I hurry to her, grab her hand and we run together while Chieng and the two boys race on. She's panting.

'I hurt my foot,' she says.

'Stay with me.Remember how you told me girls can do anything as good as boys? Well, it's true! Come on, keep going!'

I can see a stream in front of the tall tree. I know the lion can still attack us even if we're in the stream, but the water will slow it down. We reach the bank and fall into the cold rushing water. The current pulls us down and it's a few seconds before we resurface.

'Hold onto me!' I yell to Thiko as we kick and thrash to keep our heads above water. Please, God, don't let the lion cross. Let it give up and go to hunt for other prey.

Chieng, Bagic and Koko have reached the other side of the stream and are bolting out of the water for the tallest tree. Thiko and I struggle on and finally we too scramble up the bank. My skirt is soaked and heavy, clinging to my knees, and so is Thiko's. Chieng is running on ahead without looking back.

When Thiko and I reach the tree, the two little boys are already in the higher branches and Chieng is right behind them.

'Hurry! Hurry!' Koko screams, full of terror.

Thiko hoists herself up and I jump after her, grabbing a branch just as I hear the lion hit the trunk below me with his claws and his deadly power. The impact makes my toes slip but I pull myself back up and scramble higher. Thiko is just above me, and Chieng and Koko reach down for our hands and arms and pull us higher still. Koko is sobbing. Bagic hugs the trunk of the tree, his face pressed into it.

But we're safe, for now. Thiko and I are on the same branch, with Chieng opposite. We sit there listening to the lion pace below. I have to hold my knees together to stop them shaking.

'Juba,' Thiko says at last, 'how can I ever thank you? For waiting for me. That was *so* brave of you.'

'I'd face a lion a thousand times for you,' I tell her, and I'm aware of Chieng looking at me with guilt, surely thinking he shouldn't have left us behind.

We stay put and the minutes drag on. The sun burns down through the canopy. I long to be back in the water but we can go nowhere until the lion leaves. I think about how Majok once told me there was a certain stick in the forest that lions fear. I wish he'd shown me which tree it came from. If Grandpa were here, he'd have killed this lion with his spear.

Eventually the lion moves to a rise a short distance away and lies down. I can see its ribcage expanding and falling as if he's asleep. He's trying to trick us.

The sun has moved across the sky before the lion finally gets up and walks off, tail lashing one way then the other. We wait a little longer, just to be sure. When at last we decide to get down I discover that my muscles are locked. The others look as uncomfortable as I feel.

I go down first, but not all the way. I break a branch and throw it into the grass to see if it draws the lion out. We all hold still and quiet, waiting, but the only sounds are the rustling of leaves and the call of crickets and birds. The lion seems to have left. I lower myself to the ground and peer around, ready to jump back up into the tree if I have to.

I stay like that for a couple of minutes and then I'm convinced. The lion is gone.

Thiko is next down, but Chieng, Koko and Bagic are still clinging to the trunk.

'We don't want to come down,' Chieng says.

'But we agreed,' says Thiko. 'We have to keep moving. Look, it's okay. Juba and I did it. Now it's your turn.'

There's no response from the tree. Thiko looks at me, eyebrows raised. 'I thought boys were supposed to be brave,' she says.

'I heard that!' Chieng shouts. 'You're a girl, by the way!'

'And yet I'm not the one who won't come down from the tree. You're afraid, aren't you?' Thiko says.

'I'm not afraid!'

'Then be a man and come down.'

Chieng peers at her, a hard look on his face. 'You better watch your mouth,' he says.

But Thiko's taunting has worked. Chieng climbs down and Koko and Bagic follow.

'Let's get going,' I say.

Koko falls in step beside me. 'Are we going to be safe?' he whispers.

I squeeze his shoulder and tell him the only thing I can. 'Yes, Koko. We're going to be safe.'

The sun is lowering now, reflecting off the surface of the stream. We all take a long drink and I wash my wounds, and the cuts on Koko's knee and hand. Then we keep walking, on the same side of the stream and close to it. Vultures follow us, circling high above. This is a bad omen. They're waiting for one of us to drop dead so they can feast.

The further we walk, the more the landscape changes. We pass through grassy areas with few trees, then areas dense with trees and no tall grass. Then we come to a place where the land lies before us like a divine fingerprint, curving around short trees and bushes, and beyond the wall of green is a mountain.

When we reach the foot of the mountain we find a cave. A few trees twist out of one side, with leaves as hard as thorns. It's a good place to spend the night but we don't know what else might be spending the night here.

Chieng picks up a stone and throws it inside. It echoes as it lands and four bats fly out. We wait, and when nothing else appears we go in. The ground crunches beneath our feet and it feels as if we're walking on tiny bones. The cave seems to curve its way like a snake deeper into the mountain, but we don't want to go in too far. The darkness further in is like an invisible force, waiting to squeeze the life out of us.

We try to make ourselves comfortable, huddling together to keep the cold at bay. I miss the presence of the moon. I take Thiko's hand. I know she's afraid of the dark.

'It'll be okay,' I whisper, and she squeezes my hand.

It isn't long before the sound of heavy breathing coming from Chieng, Koko and Bagic tells me they're fast asleep. My own eyelids grow heavy.

'I can't believe you weren't going to tell us about Waterman,' Thiko says in as low a voice as possible. 'And I can't believe he's dead.'

'I'm sorry. I just didn't want to scare everyone. I would have told you privately.'

'So you're okay with scaring me?' Her tone is lighter now.

'I know it's hard to scare you! Except with the dark. And I don't want to keep secrets from you.'

'That's good,' Thiko says. 'We should never keep secrets from each other.'

She falls quiet for a while.

'So did Waterman actually get eaten by the lion? Did you see it?'

'No. We both just ran, in opposite directions.' I don't want to tell Thiko more. I don't want to hear those noises again in my head. I never even want to think about those awful noises again.

'What do you think is going to happen to us, Juba?'

'I don't know,' I say, trying not to sound desperate. 'We just have to keep believing that we'll find people from Pacong soon. And that our family will be among them. And we'll all make it to the refugee camp.' I'm not sure how much of this I believe myself.

Thiko's hand is warm in mine even though the rest of me is shivering. Something crawls over my shoulder and I brush it off.

'I'm glad we're together at least,' she says, her voice thick with tiredness now.

'Me too.' I'm so tired myself but it's difficult to let sleep take hold when there are bugs crawling over me. First the one on my shoulder, then another. Or maybe the same one has landed on my neck. Now it feels like there's one crawling down my back. I try to swat it away but it's out of reach. I'm about to ask Thiko if she's still awake, if she can get the bug off me, when a sharp burning pierces my flesh.

I yelp and scoot away. I know that sensation: scorpion. I twist around frantically but still can't get it off.

'What, what?' Thiko is leaping to her feet.

Chieng and the boys are awake now, saying groggily, 'Huh?'

'Scorpion!' I shriek. Then somehow I brush it off. I hear it hit the ground and scuttle away in the darkness.

Chieng and the boys bolt out of the cave. Thiko urges me to follow them, but the pain is spreading rapidly as the poison courses through my bloodstream, and my limbs don't want to work. Thiko manages to drag me outside and under a tree.

'Sit,' she says.

'I don't know if I can,' I gasp. My muscles feel like they're locked in a spasm, like they're about to explode.

Gently but firmly she pushes me down. The pain settles in my groin. My skin is boiling. I writhe on the ground, moaning, near tears. I bite back the bloodcurdling scream I want to unleash, thinking of the wild animals or the soldiers that could be lurking.

'Shh,' says Thiko, and I close my eyes to try to escape the pain. My legs shake, my teeth are clattering. I will go crazy if I don't stay calm. I want to stop shaking but the pain makes it hard to. My stomach is cold. I want to sleep. I want to dream – nice safe dreams. I think of the greenness of the fields of Pacong, the rolling brown hills baking beneath a spring sun, the giggling of happy children in the marketplace, the warm Nile breeze caressing me. Then I am in bed, curled beneath my blankets, Mama's cool hand on my forehead. Mama hugs me and kisses the top of my head.

When I wake it's light and the pain has subsided some. My back still hurts but it's tolerable. Sometimes a scorpion bite can be fatal, but I know it's not very common.

'Do you think you can get up?' Thiko asks. She wipes her palm gently across my forehead, eyes full of concern.

I stretch one leg, then the other. My muscles have relaxed a bit. My skin doesn't boil as much. Thiko helps me to my feet and at last the five of us set off, doing our best to avoid things that bite and sting. Chieng keeps asking if I'm okay and it wears on my patience.

'I'm fine,' I snap.

But a few minutes later he asks again. 'How do you feel? Do you want to stop?'

'No,' I say. 'I don't want to stop. We need to keep going.'

He nods, as if this time my answer is acceptable. We walk on, although our pace is slow.

'Juba?' Chieng says. 'You okay? You don't look good.'

I glare at him without answering. I know he's feeling guilty but his way of trying to make up for it is irritating.

We walk for a long time without a word passing between Chieng and me. The pain in my back returns in waves. One moment it feels like it's almost gone and then it starts up again. When dusk falls we find a clearing and Chieng starts a fire.

The flames grow high, licking at the darkness. They keep us warm but do nothing to sate our hunger. We haven't come across anything to eat all day. I try not to think about how good a piece of chicken would be right now.

When we're ready to sleep we gather leaves and pile them together for makeshift pillows. I lie down with my eyes wide open. No matter how hard I try, I can't relax. We've lurched from one danger to the next. So far we've managed to stay alive, but how long can we keep being lucky? What if tonight the soldiers find us? We haven't heard any gunfire today but that doesn't mean we're safe.

As if she can hear my thoughts, Thiko says, 'You know, even though we've escaped the government soldiers, there are still rebel soldiers around here. Do you ever think about that?'

Chieng isn't asleep yet either. 'If it's the rebels I'll join them,' he says. 'If it's the government soldiers I'll fight to the death.'

Thiko snorts. 'No you won't, Chieng.'

'You don't think I'm brave enough?' he says, indignant.

'If you were, you wouldn't be here with us,' I say.

'Oh, what a surprise, you're taking Thiko's side.' Chieng turns over, his back facing us.

Thiko takes my hand and gives it a squeeze. I like how holding hands has become a regular thing between us. I smile up at the starry mess above. The moon is bright in the middle of the sky, casting a milky glow across everything.

Thiko is gone when I wake next morning. The other three are still asleep. I sit up, rubbing the sleep from my eyes, but I can't see her anywhere.

I go over to Chieng and nudge him with my foot. He stirs but doesn't open his eyes. I nudge him harder.

'Let me sleep,' he mumbles.

'You have to get up, Thiko is missing.' I look around again. 'Thiko!' I call.

And just as Chieng is getting to his feet, we hear a rustling and Thiko bursts out from the bushes with a smile on her face.

'Berries!' she cries. 'I've found berries! Come on!'

That wakes Koko and Bagic, and we follow Thiko to the berries. We stuff them into our mouths as we pick them, juice dripping down our chins.

'I don't think anything I've ever eaten has tasted this good,' I say between mouthfuls.

'I know, but don't eat too many,' Thiko says. 'You'll get sick. Pace yourself.'

'But they're so good,' Chieng says, his own mouth full.

Koko and Bagic are eating just as quickly and finally Thiko says, 'No more,' and blocks their hands as they reach for the berries. 'We can take some with us.'

The last time I had fruit like this was many months ago, and I was with Majok, after school. I wonder where he is right now.

'Do you guys think Majok is okay?' I ask Thiko and Chieng.

'Yes,' Thiko says immediately.

'I have a bad feeling about him,' I say, and it's not until the words are out of my mouth that I realise I have this feeling.

'What kind of bad?' Chieng asks.

'I'm not sure.' I shake my head. 'But we can't all have made it. There's no way all our friends and family can have escaped.'

Thiko and Chieng exchange looks. They don't want to believe me. And while a part of me would love to be blindly hopeful, I know it's just not possible that we're all safe. If Grandpa can die, and Momo, and all those people whose bodies I stumbled over as I made my way from the village . . . I try not to think about Mama and Nyanbuot and Thon.

We gather as many berries as we can fit in Thiko's pack and head off. We need to find water now, but we've left the stream behind us.

'Everyone look and listen for an eagle or crest cranes,' I say.

'Why?' asks Koko.

'They nest close to water. If we see or hear one of them, water might not be far off.'

We walk until the sun is halfway across the earth, then Koko and Bagic start to fall behind. It's hot. We stop and wait for them to catch up, but it's not long before one of them has fallen behind again. This happens repeatedly, even after we've taken a long break.

'They can't keep up,' Thiko says. 'We'll have to carry them.'

Chieng looks at her warily. 'I'm not carrying them,' he says. 'Maybe if they can't keep up, we'll have to leave them behind.'

'What?' I say. I can't believe he's said this. 'We're not leaving them behind, Chieng!'

'Well, I don't know if I can even keep going myself, I don't see how you expect me to carry one of them. Why don't you carry them?'

I'm still struggling from the scorpion bite but I say nothing. I try not to look as disgusted as I feel. We're all footsore and exhausted, but Chieng is acting like he's the only one suffering.

'I'm sorry to say this,' he says, 'but I don't believe we'll survive this journey.'

What is there to say to that? Neither Thiko nor I make any reply. It's too easy to think like Chieng but I can't let myself. I can't let those thoughts gain a foothold, no matter how high the odds are stacked against us. I have to resist them or I won't be able to keep going either.

I give Chieng the berries to carry and Thiko and I carry the boys, Koko on her back with his arms wrapped around her neck, Bagic on mine. Our pace slows considerably, but we're still making more progress than when we had to keep stopping and waiting for them.

When it gets dark we find a good tree for the night. We share the rest of the berries and make ourselves as comfortable as possible. Thiko is a few branches above me and there will be no hand-holding tonight. Through the branches, a single star gleams back at me.

When dawn breaks, we climb down and continue on our way. My back is stiff and my legs feel like they might cramp up at any moment. Neither Thiko nor I are capable of carrying the boys. Thiko takes the lead and Koko and Bagic wobble along between her and me, Chieng following last. We walk through the hottest part of the day. The soles of my feet are split, the skin has been rubbed raw. My toes ache with every step.

We continue on in this way for several days, until we lose track of how many have passed. Thiko and I take turns carrying the boys and letting them walk on their own, and even Chieng carries them sometimes. We eat what little food we find, we sleep wherever we can, we grow wearier. All our spirits are flagging now, and at times there are arguments. We patch them up and stumble on.

Early one afternoon, when Thiko is again in the lead, she suddenly stops and puts up a hand for silence. I hold my breath as we listen. At first I hear nothing out of the ordinary but then – it sounds like voices. Coming from up ahead of us.

We hurry forward as quietly as we can. It's not possible to tell what language is being spoken. Thiko and I peer nervously around a bend in the path, holding the two boys back.

Up ahead a group of people are gathered. Maybe fifty or so, mostly women and children.

My relief is almost unbearable. These people are surrounded by rough bundles, not guns. Then I recognise some of them.

'They're from Pacong!' I cry, springing out and rushing towards them, Thiko and the others following.

The villagers all turn and look at us, spooked themselves now, perhaps thinking *we* might be soldiers. But they relax as soon as they see us. I scan their faces but I don't see Mama. I ask if anyone has seen her, or my brother and sister, but no one has. No one has any news of them.

Chieng wanders among the group, looking for his own family. A woman with two small children recognises Koko and Bagic and motions them to her. I can tell by the eager way they tumble all over her that they are relatives. She brushes tears from Bagic's eyes and hugs them both close.

'I'll take care of you until we find your mama,' she tells them.

Thiko too has been asking after her mother with no success. My heart shrinks. After feeling such elation on finding the villagers I fling myself onto the grass and hug my knees. If Mama isn't here it means I'll never see her again. I will never again see Thon or Nyanbuot either.

But then Thiko scoots close and rubs my back and I think how I am not alone. I wonder how she can be so strong.

'Try not to think too much right now,' she says. 'If we're okay, chances are our families are too. There'll be other groups, somewhere else. We'll find them.'

'I should have done something. Back in Pacong.'

'Done what?' she asks. 'Juba, what could you have possibly done?'

'I don't know. Anything. *Something*.'

'You did what you could. You survived. Now what you have to do is keep your hope alive. Because without it we're as weak and fragile as grass in a summer fire.'

I stare at her.

'My mama says that,' she tells me quietly.

7

We're discussing our next move when, without warning, men in uniform are surrounding us. Not government soldiers, but rebels from the People's Liberation Army. In the excitement of our two groups meeting each other, no one heard their stealthy approach.

The air thickens with fear. The men move among our group with rifles and angry words. They might leave us alone when they see we don't have any goats, I think hopefully. They might even show us the way to the refugee camp. I search their faces – maybe Deng is among them.

'Everyone on your feet!' one of them shouts. 'Now!'

I scramble up beside Thiko and the rebels herd us together.

I don't know what they want. I have nothing. The other villagers have only meagre possessions. I'm scared they're looking for recruits, and that Chieng and I might be taken.

One weary villager, Majak, who lived on the eastern side of Pacong, has remained sitting with his head in his hands, ignoring the orders to stand.

'You, get up!' shouts a soldier, prodding him with his rifle. 'Coward! Why are you running away like a woman? Why haven't you joined the rebels to fight?'

Majak stares up at him with tired red eyes and says nothing. I don't know what's wrong with him, or why he doesn't obey. It can only mean trouble.

For a moment the soldier looks like he's about to walk away but then he turns, pulls out his knife and stabs Majak in the stomach. Majak has made no effort to defend himself and now he just lets go, as if that's what he wanted all along.

Thiko covers her face with her hands. I stand as still as possible, not drawing attention to myself, just gazing at Majak lying there with blood pooling beneath him. His eyes are open and staring at nothing.

'All of you, put out your possessions!' his killer shouts.

I look over to see Koko and Bagic shaking in terror as the rebels search through the villagers' bundles, dumping out the pitiful contents. They take any water bottles they see.

'Where are all the good-looking girls?' one rebel yells. 'Who will bear our children for us if you all run away? Who will come after to keep fighting this war?'

Next to me Thiko trembles. I take her hand but she just keeps staring straight ahead.

A few yards from us a rebel rests his hand on the shoulder of a girl. She flinches at his touch. He smiles creepily when she does this and then he grabs her roughly and drags her away.

'No!' the girl's mother screams, trying to hold onto her daughter. Another soldier brings the barrel of his rifle down on the woman's back and she staggers, losing her grip. Tears stream down her face but she does not cry out again as she watches the soldier disappear with her daughter.

I have turned numb. How can we have made it so far and survived so much, and found our people, only for this to happen?

Someone is tugging at my arm. A soldier, grinning at me, showing his crooked yellow teeth.

'You,' he says. 'Come with me.'

I try to yank my arm back. 'No! I'm not a girl!'

He leers. 'Then why are you wearing a skirt?'

'Look, I'm a boy!' I lift the skirt. 'I didn't have anything else to wear.'

The soldier laughs cruelly. 'A boy in a skirt, eh?' His leery gaze shifts to Thiko. 'And what about this one? You, I can tell you're a girl.'

'I might be a girl but I'm not well,' Thiko snaps. 'I would make you ill. Very ill.'

I say a quick hard prayer that they will believe her. But even if they don't, I will not let her go with them, no matter what.

Thiko pulls out her filthy handkerchief, caked with dirt and dried blood. She coughs into it violently and holds it up to the soldier's face, shaking it at him. 'Do you see? I will make you sick!'

The soldier looks uncertain for a second and then pushes her aside in disgust. I'm about to let out a sigh of relief when he wheels around and slaps her, sending her head flying backwards. 'That doesn't make me sick,' he snarls.

'Stop it!' I yell, throwing myself between him and Thiko.

He grins his ugly grin again. 'Ah, now the boy is trying to be a man. Too bad you're failing miserably. Here's your first lesson in manhood: men don't wear skirts.' He leans in close to me and I can smell his rotten breath. 'But little baby girls do.'

His buddies roar as if he's said the funniest thing ever. All that matters to me is that he's walking away, he's actually walking away and Thiko is safe.

'Are you okay?' I ask. She's trembling, drenched in sweat. Already I can see swelling under her eye.

She says nothing. I follow her gaze to another young girl being dragged away.

'I'm okay,' Thiko says. 'But those girls are not.'

From the bushes come cries, angry yelling, the sound of slapping. Now Ajak, a woman known in the village for brewing the best beer, pushes her way through the soldiers and shouts, 'Leave them alone, you're acting like animals!'

I look away, not wanting to see what will happen. I focus on two crested cranes dancing on an anthill in the distance.

But they don't shoot Ajak. She reappears moments later carrying a crying girl. It's not her daughter. Even though Ajak is married she never had children.

'Shh,' Ajak says, 'you're going to be alright. We'll leave soon.'

Another of the rebels has been sizing me up and now he comes over.

'You,' he says, 'why aren't you a soldier? You're old enough.'

I can't think what to say. I don't want them to take me away, like they maybe took Deng.

When I stay silent the rebel gives me a look. 'So, you're wondering why we're doing this?' he says.

I nod, too afraid to speak.

'It's because all this,' he sweeps his arm around at the land, 'is our home. It's where we live. Our food, our clothes, our medicine, and yes, even our women, come from the civilians. People hate us for this, but we want to liberate our country. To do that, we have to survive, like everybody else.'

'I understand,' I say, although I don't really. Then I summon the courage to ask, 'Will we be able to go back to our village soon?'

'Do you think you can fight if I give you a gun?'

I freeze again. Beside me Thiko says, 'No, he's a coward. He's scared of fighting.'

The rebel says, 'Let me ask you, do you like your village?'

'I love my village. That's where I first opened my eyes.'

'Then if you love it so much, pick up an AK and fight for it. That's the only way you'll get it back.'

A whistle sounds, their signal to leave. The rebel straightens and looks at me again.

'Be careful,' he says. 'The jungle is infested with government soldiers looking for runaways.' He walks off with his laughing friends.

I watch him go, stunned. He doesn't seem like the other rebels. I wonder why he gave me that advice. And why they've let me stay, Chieng too. Too late I realise that I should have asked him if he knew anything about Deng.

Our group continues on. It's a wonder we have the strength to keep walking, but we do. We walk by day and hide at night, taking turns to carry the children. We are a sorry bunch, wounded and sore, bereaved, half starved. Some days we have nothing to eat but leaves. They are bitter and hard to chew and they stick in your throat like wood, but it's something in our bellies. We don't talk much now, we don't have the energy for it, but at least Thiko and Chieng and I are among adults. We no longer bear sole responsibility for Koko and Bagic. This is a big relief.

When we approach a valley one afternoon my spirits lift, but as we get closer I see it is bare. The grass stands lifelessly under the relentless sun. The ground is hard and cracked beneath our feet.

One day we see more rebel soldiers in the distance, walking in our direction, and quickly we hide, urging the little ones to stay quiet. The soldiers stop not far from us and stand there talking. They study the ground.

'People have been here just recently,' I hear one of them say, and my stomach knots. Will they decide to trace our footprints?

The soldier who spoke leaves the group and walks our way. We hold our breath. But he stops suddenly, pulls his pants down and squats. He farts like a pregnant pig. When he's done relieving himself, he pulls up his pants and goes back to his group. They continue on their way.

A day later we come across a tangle of burnt-out jeeps.

'The government soldiers must have fought the rebels here,' a woman says.

Among the wreckage a tin of food is found. Someone else finds a water container. I'm hoping to find something useful too, but it's not food or water I turn up, it's one of our Pacong neighbours, who volunteered to fight alongside the rebels. He is lying there with his legs gone. His arms are thrown up over his head, like a dancer. It's almost comical in its horror and suddenly I can't stop giggling.

'Why are you laughing?' Thiko asks.

I show her. 'It's like he's dancing,' I say, between my laughter. 'Except how can he, when he doesn't have any legs?'

'That's not funny!' she snaps. 'Not funny at all!' She steps away from me and I see a fearful look in her eyes. It's not because of the dead man or the soldiers, it's because of me. But I just can't stop laughing, even though I want to. Thiko steps back in close and slaps my face hard and I stop.

'You're in shock,' she says. 'Come away from here now.' And she pulls me after her.

Later I'm horrified that I laughed like that. Nothing could be less funny.

One night we wake to the sound of gunfire and screaming. Darkness hides whatever dreadful thing is upon us now, but soldiers are shooting at us, that much I know. They want more dead bodies. People are scrambling up and running away, tripping over each other. The dark is as thick as a curtain.

As usual I've been lying near Thiko, with Chieng not far from us, and now we're all fleeing, unsure where we're going. We wrestle through bushes and low trees, branches that scratch at our arms and legs. My lungs burn. It feels as though I can't take in oxygen fast enough.

Thiko is snagged by a branch and I stop to help. Then she gives a shriek. 'Something bit my arm!'

My eyes have adjusted enough to see a snake twisting its way up a branch. Thiko sinks to the ground, crying and holding her arm.

I sit down and take her head in the crook of my arm, but only for a moment. I tear a strip off the bottom of her skirt that I'm wearing, which is already close to rags, and tie it firmly over her arm so the poison won't spread as quickly. Chieng helps me massage the area where she was bitten, to try to squeeze the poison out.

After a minute or so he says, 'Juba, we need to go. We can't stay here. We'll get left behind. We'll be on our own again.' The bushes around us are rustling with people running through.

'Thiko,' I say, 'we have to get you up.'

'I don't know if I can,' she wails.

'You *can*,' I say fiercely. 'You can do anything as good as we can, remember?'

We help her up and put her good arm across my shoulder, but she struggles to stand. I try to get her onto my back but we both fall to the ground.

'We can leave her here and go get help,' Chieng suggests.

'Help from where? We can't leave her alone!'

'No, Chieng is right,' Thiko mumbles. Sweat runs down her face and her head lolls against me. 'I'm slowing you down. Go ahead without me.'

'I'll find help.' Chieng takes off without looking behind to see if I'm following.

'Juba . . .' Thiko says.

'Shh,' I say. 'Don't talk. Save your energy.'

'You have to go.'

Voices are shouting not far off. I grip her shoulders and she raises her head. Her eyes glow. 'Come on,' I urge, 'we need to go.'

'*You* need to. We can't both make it.' A look of acceptance spreads over her face. 'But you can.'

'You just have to let me get you onto my back,' I say. 'Then I'll carry you.'

'No, we already tried. You have to run.'

I shut out visions of Pacong, and Grandpa telling me the same thing. The shouting is closer now. In the gloom I can make out a bright orange flicker. Then gunshots echo through the trees.

'I'm not leaving you, Thiko. Chieng will find help.' I'm not sure I really believe that last bit.

I wrap her arms around my neck and pick her up and manage to carry her into the cover of a thick bush. I get her settled and see that her arm has swelled alarmingly.

'I'm tired,' she says. 'I want to sleep.'

'No, Thiko, you must stay awake!' I remember Grandpa saying that if you're bitten by a snake and fall asleep you might never wake up again. I give Thiko a shake.

'I'm so tired ...'

'It's okay, Thiko,' I say, gently slapping her face. 'I'm here. You're going to be okay. Don't go to sleep now. Listen to my voice and stay awake. Stay here with me.' And I start gabbling like a madman, saying anything that comes into my mind, anything to stop her falling asleep. She stays awake but continues to tremble. The gunfire stops at last and the moon has appeared from behind clouds, and as I talk I peer out into the night, hoping against hope that Chieng will return with someone who can help.

And then, just as I'm growing panicky, help comes. Not in the form of a person, but a tree. Only a few yards off. If finding Thiko after the attack on Pacong was a miracle, here is the second one. I don't know the name of this tree but when my eyes land on it I recognise it. Grandpa once pointed out such a tree in our garden.

I immediately wonder if my mind is playing tricks on me, but I tell Thiko that I'm leaving her for a second.

'I'm only going over there, just a little way. I'm not leaving for good, okay? I'll be right over there and I'm going to get something that will help you. Did you hear me?'

'Yes. Okay.' I can barely hear her.

I crawl out from under the bush, hurry over to the tree and break off a dry branch and use it to dig out a piece from the roots. I split it back and peel off the inside part and bring it to Thiko. I help her sit up and her body is heavy against mine.

'Thiko, I'm going to put something in your mouth and you have to chew it, okay? Chew it well and quickly. It will make you better.'

She opens her mouth and takes the piece of root but her jaw doesn't seem to work. 'I want to sleep,' she says, the piece falling out of her mouth. Her eyes roll back in her head.

I slap her cheeks and shake her. 'Thiko! You *must* stay awake.' I grab the root and put it in my mouth, chewing it hard, squeezing the juice from it, then I open her mouth again and cover it with my own. I force the juice into her mouth and massage her throat and her head jerks to the side, but she's swallowed some of it. I repeat the process, getting more juice into her. Her body goes rigid and after a few seconds she vomits a foamy substance.

I hold her by the shoulders. 'It's okay, Thiko, it's good. You're getting rid of the poison.' I feel dizzy now, from chewing on the root. It would help if I could vomit myself, but I can't. So I sit there and hold Thiko, who keeps vomiting.

We stay like that through the night. When the sun rises I see that her arm is twice its normal size. It looks very painful. But she's alive. I have never seen a more beautiful sight.

'How are you feeling?' I ask.

'Tired. Can't I sleep now?'

'Yes. I think you're past the danger point.'

I help her out from the bush and heap leaves under her as a mattress. She's asleep when her head reaches the ground. I prop myself against the tree trunk next to her and doze off myself.

When we wake, the sun says it's late afternoon. Chieng has not come back. We're alone.

'Can you walk?' I ask.

'I think so.' She looks at her arm. The swelling has reduced. It's just around the area that was bitten now.

I help her up. The joints in my knees crack and my back is sore. But we need to keep moving, even if we only cover a short distance before dark. We can't let our group get any further ahead of us.

We take frequent breaks as we walk. Thiko is thirsty from all the vomiting, but the sun sets without us finding water. And without us seeing Chieng or any of the others. The only thing we come across is the carcass of an elephant. It lies with its face and tusks hacked off.

We shelter for the night in a large bush, nestling deep under the foliage for cover. A hyena barks nearby and another answers.

Thiko shudders. 'They're close.'

'They are. I'll try to light a fire to keep them off. You stay here.'

I scramble out from the bush, find dry wood and grass and make a firestick. I have to rub for a long time before there's a spark, then longer until a small flame shoots up. I hold it to my little pile of dry grass and twigs and it licks hungrily. Soon there's a warm glow and I pile on wood. There's no sound now from the hyenas.

I call Thiko and she comes to sit by the fire with me. It's so soothing to be near a fire and I start to feel sleepy. Then I see something flickering in the distance.

'What's that?' I point at the tiny lights and Thiko squints.

'Fireflies?'

'That's what I thought, but I'm not sure.'

'Juba, it could be those soldiers again!'

We strain our ears for any sound of shouting men but can hear nothing.

'I'm going to see what it is,' I say. 'I won't sleep if I think it's soldiers, and if it is, they'll have seen our fire. You wait here.'

'Oh no, I'm coming with you,' she says, getting to her feet.

'Thiko, you're still weak. You should stay here. I'll keep out of sight and come back for you.'

'Don't argue with me, you won't win. I'm coming.'

I sigh. I know she's right.

So I take her hand and we keep low as we move towards the lights. As we get closer they become flames. So it is a fire. We creep forward a little more and then I pull Thiko into a bush and we peer out. There are people warming themselves around the fire. They don't look like soldiers. We take a few more steps and a twig snaps loudly. The people round the fire turn and look our way, eyes filled with fear.

Then the impossible happens.

I see Nyanbuot. I see my sister. I blink, not sure I can trust my eyes. But it *is* her! She's filthy and her face is scratched and her hair is wild, but it's Nyanbuot.

I run to her and she jumps up and flies at me like a human missile, straight into my arms. And right behind her comes Mama.

We just stand there hugging each other for the longest time. Both of them are crying, their arms tight around me. I want to cry too but I don't let myself.

Then comes even more happiness. Thiko's mother is here too. 'I knew you would find me,' she says, over and over again as she clasps her daughter. 'I knew you would find me . . .'

When we finally let go of each other I look Mama over. She is thin. She has grey hairs I don't remember, her face is lined and weary. But none of that matters. She's alive. She and Nyanbuot. We are together again.

Thiko and her mother move away to greet others. 'Where's Thon?' I ask, looking around the group.

Mama doesn't answer. Nyanbuot clings to me as though I'm a ghost that will disappear any moment. Mama takes my hand.

My stomach goes cold.

'Sit,' Mama says and I obey, Nyanbuot still holding onto me.

'He was innocent, our Thon,' Mama begins. 'A child. Impetuous, lazy most of the time, but these things we forgive. He is in a better place now.'

I can hardly take this in. My little brother. We've already lost Deng, and my father, and now Thon is dead too? A part of me seems to die as well. I've gone from being unbelievably happy to the very opposite. I'm the only male left in our family and I know I must be strong for Mama, for my sister, but it's so hard.

I put my arm around Mama's shoulders.

'We walked for many days,' she says. 'We looked for you everywhere. We asked everyone we came across if they'd seen you or Grandpa or Momo.'

I can't stop my tears now. I nod, and say nothing about Grandpa or Momo. Not yet.

'Thon did his best to entertain us,' Mama continues, 'to try to keep our spirits up. He made his funny faces – you know how he was. And he minded himself very well. When we had to hide from soldiers he was still as a mouse. He'd run ahead to look for water. Do you know what he'd say? "I'm going to be as fast a runner as Juba one day. If he was here now, he would run ahead. I'm a big boy now, I will do it too." And he'd take off. And sometimes he did find water. He even found an abandoned canteen once and filled it at a waterhole.'

Now I'm smiling while I'm crying. I had always known that Thon looked up to me, even if he rarely showed it.

'How did he die?' I ask Mama.

'He fell sick, we don't know what from, and the poor child just got weaker and weaker,' she says. 'We carried him, but there was nothing else we could do for him. Then one morning . . . he just didn't wake up.'

By the time I stop crying I'm so exhausted it's all I can do to make up a rough sleeping place before I fall instantly asleep. I lie next to Nyanbuot and Mama and I sleep better than I have for days.

In the morning, Mama stares at me oddly. 'Juba,' she says, 'why are you wearing a skirt?'

'Oh,' I say, 'I'm so used to it now I've forgotten about it.' And I tell her and Nyanbuot what happened. Then, to make them laugh,

I prance around, swirling Thiko's tattered old skirt this way and that. They burst into giggles and it's beautiful music.

I keep hamming it up until finally Mama brings out her pack.

'Look inside,' she says.

I do, and find a pair of my own pants and a shirt. I can't keep the grin off my face as I hold them up.

'Mama! How did you manage to pack these?' I pull them on and it feels so good to be in clean clothes. And I'm a boy again.

Mama can't stop smiling now either. 'I knew we would find each other. That's why I have those clothes. I never gave up hope that we would find you.'

I give her a long hug. 'Thank you, Mama.'

Thiko runs up and grabs my hands. 'You have pants!' she exclaims. 'And see, I'm wearing a clean skirt.' We jump up and down. We laugh. We dance in a circle. 'I found my mother and you found your family,' she sings.

Then she stops suddenly and turns sad. 'Except for Thon. My mother told me. Oh Juba, I'm so sorry.' She goes to speak to Mama, to offer condolences. And we're all silent for a long time. I've never felt so sad and so happy at the same time.

There are a lot more people in this group than the last one. I know many of their faces, but there are many more I've never seen before. No one seems to be talking much. They speak with their eyes or nod their heads. I don't know if it's because they're tired, or grieving for what they've lost, or fearful of their unknown future. I remember those days in school when I wanted the class to be quiet and let me think in peace. How I long for that noisy classroom now.

There's movement as everyone gets ready for the day's walk. And there's more good news: it seems we are not far from the refugee camp. We may even reach it today.

We set off, and as we walk, more people join us. I look for Chieng, and for Majok. Maybe they're already at the camp. It's almost too exciting to think about.

It's strange to be back among so many people. We're like the Israelites roaming the desert, seeking the land of milk and honey.

Towards midday Thiko, who's gone on ahead of us, comes racing back down the path, her face illuminated. 'Juba!' she shouts. 'Look who I found!'

Behind her come Chieng and Majok, both grinning from ear to ear. We grip each other by the shoulders and I can't wipe the grin off my own face. I don't even care that Chieng abandoned Thiko and me – we're together now, we've made it this far, and if we can do that we can make it all the way. It feels like nothing bad will happen to us again.

'I found Majok after I left you,' Chieng says, 'and we went back to get you both.' He's breathless, his words spilling out in haste. 'But we couldn't find you anywhere. We looked and looked, and then we had to go back or we'd lose our group.'

I don't know if this is true or not but I nod. 'It's alright. We must have taken different paths.'

'That brought us all to the same place,' Thiko says happily.

Majok doesn't look too bad, although like all of us he's filthy and thin. And sad around the eyes. He tells me his father didn't make it out of Pacong and he's not hopeful about his mother either, because one of her legs is shorter than the other and she limps. He's praying his sister is alive and already in the camp.

Mama roughs up his hair, as she does with mine sometimes. 'It's good to see both of you boys,' she says. 'Have you found any of your own family, Chieng?'

'Two cousins. But maybe my mother and the others will be at the camp. They say we'll be there today if we walk fast, and there'll be food and fresh water for everyone.'

Hearing these words puts a spring in our step. Food and fresh water. A safe place to sleep. It's all any of us want right now. Apart from our missing family members.

'You'll find your family, Chieng,' I say. 'They'll be waiting for you in the camp.'

We march on. A giraffe stands tall and proud with its long neck in an acacia tree, a pure animal spirit alive under the sun. A couple of hours later I look ahead and see dark fences stretching before us.

From behind someone shouts, 'It's the camp!'

Part Two

1

We stand on the hill and stare down at the rows of white tents below. Countless of them. I've never seen anything like this. I wonder how many people are living here and what their life is like. What my life will be like. I marvel at the fact that we've made it. Despite everything, here we are, after walking on our aching feet for such a long way. We've travelled 450 miles, someone in our group says.

I can feel the fear and worry fall away. It is the promised land after all. Mama looks as if she can hardly believe her eyes either. She too has suddenly relaxed.

Beside me are Chieng and Majok and Thiko, as happy as I am. And then, even though we've just walked so far, and our bodies and feet are full of pain, I can't resist. 'Race you!' I shout, and we tear away, kicking up dust.

It's like we're back in the village, like this is any old day and we're racing home from school. The bombings never happened, everyone is still alive. Thiko and Majok fall behind, leaving Chieng and me neck and neck. Little by little I pull ahead. Then I remember that he's not yet found any family and I pretend to stumble, slowing enough for him to overtake me.

'Beat you!' he says, grinning madly when we reach the gates. 'That's a first.'

We pant as we wait for the others to join us. We want to go through together.

At the gate are five men in uniform, with blue helmets that look like Mama's soup bowl. They're UN soldiers, I learn. The camp is protected by a barbed-wire fence but it's falling apart in places, with shreds of plastic bags clinging to it. We peer through it into the camp.

Every inch of ground is covered, with tents, people, belongings. And garbage, I can now see. Garbage seems to be strewn all through the camp. Further inside, people are waiting in line for something. There are several lines and they're long. I can't see their end or their beginning. Other people are putting up makeshift shelters of bark and twigs. Some are just sitting on the ground and staring at nothing, it seems.

Now that I'm up close I suddenly feel differently about the camp. And I can see Thiko thinking the same. Then Nyanbuot reaches us and she doesn't appear to like the look of it either.

Thiko gives me a slight nod as if to say, We can do this. So I smile and pat Nyanbuot's head and try to look confident as the rest of our group join us.

When everyone is there, one of the UN soldiers motions us through the double gates. He seems to have no energy in his arm, as if he's tired of doing this for the whole day. Some people hurry through eagerly, others hang back warily, but once inside we all end up moving like a shoal of fish. There's nobody to tell us where we should go, we just walk through never-ending rows of tents that look as flimsy as cardboard. There are children chasing each other and squealing with laughter, but other children are lethargic, sitting in groups with flies clustering around their eyes and nostrils. We pass a little boy lying on the ground just as he vomits, and a girl, maybe his sister, tries to get him to sit up.

The sun burns down. People squeeze into the shade cast by the tents, some watching their children play, some just staring into space. I wonder nervously if I will like living here.

I walk with Mama and Nyanbuot and eventually our group comes across someone who leads us to an office building, where a white man comes out to meet us. The concrete wall of the building looks like it's just been painted, in yellow and brown. There are more UN soldiers outside the building.

The white man talks quickly in English. He sounds like he has a lot to do. 'We've been trying to get everyone to register,' he tells us, 'but we're filling up quickly.'

My stomach drops. Are they going to turn us away?

'But there's still space available,' he goes on. 'Can you form a line, please, over there by that table.' He points to where we should go. 'Once you're done you can get settled in.'

The table is a long rickety thing with a number of African people and three white people sitting behind it and a long line standing in front of it. Many of them look like they've been waiting for some time. We shuffle away to take our place at the end of the line and the white man goes back inside.

No one is sure what the registration involves but whatever it is it must be complicated, because the line doesn't appear to move at all. Several people give up and wander off. Mama sees me watching them and shakes her head.

'We'll wait our turn,' she says. 'We'll do this the right way.'

The right way means waiting several hours. When we finally reach the table the woman asks our names and what village we are from and writes them on a form, then she tells us to stand to one side with a group of others and wait for a UN worker to show us where we can set up.

We can hardly believe it. We waited all this time just for it to be done so quick? I wonder why all those people before us were at the table for so long, but before we can ask any questions the woman has already moved on to the people behind us.

When the UN man arrives, our group, which includes my family, Chieng, Majok, Thiko and her mother, follows him through the maze of tents. Nathan was the only white man I ever saw up close before, but I don't want to think about him just now. I must help out where I can as we settle into this new home, if that's what it is.

We pass more piles of garbage and the air is thick with unpleasant smells. Along the paths between the rows of tents are signs, but I don't know what they mean and the rows don't seem to be in any order. We go down one row after another and I see a few more UN soldiers as we walk. I can hear moaning coming from some of the tents, where people must be sick. We come upon an old man sitting on the ground who's so skinny you can see his bones. He seems to be looking at me but I realise he's not. His face is hard, like the bark of a dead tree. He blinks, so I know he's alive, but it's like his life has moved on and left him just sitting there.

Mama grabs my arm and pulls me close. 'Stay near me,' she says. 'I don't want to lose you. I don't know how people find their way through here, every row looks the same.' She asks the man leading us how many people there are in this camp and he tells her eight hundred thousand. At first we think he's got it wrong, or we haven't heard right, but when we ask again he repeats it.

'There are people here from every tribe in South Sudan,' he says. 'This war . . .' He shakes his head. Then he tells us there are just under a thousand aid workers here, from twenty-two different organisations.

Mama holds my hand tightly and I can feel her thinking the same thing. How can there be enough food and water for so many people? I wonder whether they will place us in different tents, and what will happen with Thiko and the others.

Finally we stop at the end of a row of tents. 'Here we are,' says the UN man. 'Zone D.' Then he tells us they've run out of tents and will bring us one when they get more. 'In the meantime,' he says, 'if you could build yourselves a shelter just here.' He points to a bare patch of ground.

'But where will we sleep?' Thiko's mother asks.

'Don't worry,' he says, 'we're working on getting more tents as soon as possible. We'll have them to you as soon as they come in. Just hang tight for now.'

'What about food?' I ask. 'And water?'

He scratches his chin as if he's not sure what to tell us. 'We're working on the food too. There are two wells in this zone. You need to be prepared to wait a while for water.'

Later we discover that waiting a while often means hours at a time.

It will soon be dark. We start work immediately on a shelter. Chieng and I go to ask our neighbours if anyone has tools and eventually we have four machetes. We set off with some others to look for support sticks. About a hundred yards from where we've been told to make our shelter there are shrubs, and beyond that, jungle. The trees close in have been stripped of suitable branches and we must walk further in.

By the time we find what we need we're all exhausted, but we manage to construct a basic shelter. It's thin and surely won't keep out rain, but it's something over our heads and it isn't raining now.

We drag our meagre belongings under it, Chieng, Majok, Mama, Nyanbuot and I, along with Thiko and her mother and the rest of our little group, and fall immediately asleep.

Early next morning, Mama, Thiko's mother and some other adults are taken to the office to collect emergency rations, while Thiko and I go to look for teeth-brushing sticks. We bring handfuls back and distribute them to our group. Mama returns carrying a bundle on her head and another in her arms. When she puts them down I see that she has a scoop of maize flour, some salt and split lentils. Also a jerry can for water, a bucket and basin for washing, a solar lamp, a saucepan, some soap and sanitary pads. These are the things with which we're to start building our new life.

Thiko and Nyanbuot set off to the well and Mama and the other women look for firewood. They don't need a lot because there's not much to cook. I am appointed guard of our few precious belongings while they're gone. After we've eaten, the women collect our dirty clothes and walk the half a mile to the stream to wash them.

With nothing else to do I sit outside the shelter and watch a couple of little boys at play. A girl follows gamely behind them. She has big round eyes and a stump instead of a left arm. A grimy bandage trails from the stump like a flag of defeat but she's smiling as if she owns the world. I'm wondering if she really feels that way, when someone runs up to me. An older boy. I tense involuntarily as I recognise him. It's Bol.

But just as suddenly I realise that I'm not afraid of him anymore. I don't want to fight with him but I won't back down from him.

Bol is wearing only shorts and they are riddled with holes. He's smiling broadly. Maybe he's changed.

'Hey! It's really you, Juba!'

Part of me thinks this could be a trick and he will try to knock me down any second, but another part of me hopes we can get along. That we can put our differences behind us after everything that's happened. Those fights at school seem so pointless now.

'Bol, I'm so glad to see you!' I say. 'How are you?'

'For today I am alright,' he grins. 'I can't tell you about tomorrow, though. Tomorrow is a gift here.'

I'm not quite sure what he means by this but I don't ask. 'Well,' I say, 'I'm happy you're alright today.'

'Thanks,' he says, and just then Chieng and Majok appear. There are more greetings and smiles and Bol says how happy he is that we all made it here. He sounds sincere, like we've never been anything other than friends. I struggle to think whether he was as mean to me as I'm remembering.

'When did you get here?' I ask him.

'Four days ago.' He sweeps an arm around him. 'Four days ago this place had about half as many people. Every day more and more arrive. Where are they all coming from? How many more will show up?' He shrugs. 'They'll probably run out of ration cards soon, if they haven't already.'

'What are ration cards?' Chieng asks.

'It's how we get food and supplies,' Bol says. 'You need a ration card if you want food. Haven't you got one yet?'

We shake our heads.

'You should then. My father won't even let me touch ours. He's afraid I'll lose it.'

Bol is lucky to have all his family in the camp. He tells me that after the attack on Pacong his father was separated from his mother and siblings, and they didn't meet up again until they reached the camp.

Once Bol has left, Majok and I go with Chieng to the registration office to ask about Chieng's family. They have no record of his parents or his brothers and sisters and they tell us to go to the Red Cross office, just near the registration building.

We make our way to a portable building made of corrugated iron. It's crowded with people asking about missing persons. Some have photos to show the Red Cross workers. Chieng and I try to squeeze our way in but it's impossible. We could wait here all day, so we decide instead to go and ask around the camp.

After hours of fruitless searching, Chieng's hopes are still high, even though we've come across a lot of children who aren't with their parents, and just as many parents who don't have their children with them. I wonder why the childless parents don't pick a child to look after, at least for a while, but it doesn't seem to work that way.

I wonder, too, if these children still dream of going home. Although I'm a long way from Pacong, I could find my way back there. Grandpa taught me how to tell the direction and time of day by the position of the sun, and I know a lot of these boys would also know how to get home. But knowing your way home doesn't help much when your home is no longer there.

Heading back to our makeshift shelter we pass two old ladies. We haven't seen that many old people in the camp. Most of them wouldn't have been able to manage the long walk here, running from danger to danger. But these two have somehow made it. They look frail and delicate as moths, as though the next big gust of wind could blow them away.

After a couple of weeks our situation hasn't improved much. We still don't have a tent or a ration card. Every day the men venture into the jungle to forage. Our hunger pangs are as strong now as they were on our journey here. Even the trees are being stripped of leaves.

Mama and Nyanbuot's days are consumed by fetching water and collecting firewood to cook what little food we can scrounge, just enough that we don't starve. Chieng, Majok and I eat from one plate while Mama, Nyanbuot, Thiko and her mother eat from another. Getting water from the well has become harder every day, Mama tells me. Sometimes, if the well is too crowded, we drink the water from the stream, after first boiling it.

A fight almost breaks out one day. A few men thought someone had killed a bird and was going to roast it, but it turned out no one had a bird, it was just a baby squawking. I hear a woman tell another that the UN will send food rations from Kenya. I don't know why it's taking so long for supplies to get here. This camp is the opposite of the land of milk and honey, it's more like the land of dust and garbage.

Many people here seem to have given up the fight to survive, and I can see even Mama is starting to lose hope. It's been a while since I saw her smile. I've only ever known her to be a strong woman and I hate to see her weakening. She's a different person to the one I met on the path to the camp. It hurts me to see her just sitting on the ground staring in front of her, like that old man we saw on the first day here.

When she's not sitting and staring she spends much of her time sleeping. Nyanbuot and I can't get her to engage in anything for more than a short period. She always finds an excuse to go back to sitting and staring or sleeping. It's like she thinks if she sleeps long enough, she'll wake up warm in her own bed back in the village.

But our village, I have to keep reminding myself, has been destroyed. What is left of Pacong? The mudbrick walls of any huts still standing will crumble. The thatched roofs and fences will have succumbed to the fire, then the rain, followed by the harsh sun. I imagine the remains being baked into a flat, ugly sculpture, where once was a village full of trees, grass and wildflowers. The village of my birth is no longer my home.

Some nights Mama talks in her sleep. Two nights ago I woke up to find that she wasn't in the shelter with us. I went outside and there she was, sitting and staring at the stars. I cuddled her and said things to try to make her laugh, but it didn't work. Last night, when she thought we were all asleep, I heard her crying softly. I crept over and held her, told her everything would be alright and to go back to sleep, just the way she used to do with me. It's up to me to take care of her now.

Even Nyanbuot is helping take care of Mama more than she is expecting to be taken care of. Nyanbuot and I don't talk about the change in Mama, we only smile at each other, hoping she's still in there and someday she'll come back to us fully.

This morning I came out to find her sitting on the ground and staring again.

'I'm thinking about our village,' she says when I ask. 'Do you ever think about our village, Juba?'

'Of course I do, Mama. All the time.' I sit down next to her. 'I think about Pacong and school, about Grandpa too.' I hesitate. I've told her what happened to Grandpa and Momo and I don't want to upset her more by reminding her of it. But then I decide to tell her again how brave Grandpa was in defending me.

It's hard to look at her eyes as I talk, and saying Grandpa's name still hurts every time I say it, but I want her to know how courageous he was, and once I've started talking about him I don't want to stop. I never want to forget what a good, kind man he was.

'And,' I finish at last, 'I made myself a promise to tell his stories and keep them alive. Keep him and our village alive.'

Mama nods sadly. 'Your grandfather loved you very much, Juba.' She leans over and kisses me on the cheek.

'I know he did. I loved him too. And I miss him. But he wanted us to survive, Mama, he didn't want us to give up. We've got to keep going for him. We've got to keep our hope strong.'

She has told me so many times herself that hope is everything, but now she only sighs and goes back to staring at the ground.

It's easy enough to tell Mama to stay strong, even if saying it has no effect, but I find it hard to do myself. It's hard to stop thinking. I wonder why the most beautiful memories are the worst, cutting my insides like knives.

Groups of kids have emerged from the tents and shelters now, to run and play. Koko and Bagic, who live with their relative in another shelter, come out to play too, and I'm glad to see them so lively. I want to join in but there's an invisible rope keeping me within Mama's orbit. I've sometimes seen Nyanbuot looking longingly at a group of giggling girls, but she too stays close to Mama as much as possible.

But later that day, my sister comes running up with something in her hand.

'Juba!' she calls excitedly, and shows me what she has. It's a bunch of slender twigs tied together with leaves and bark to make a doll. Nyanbuot hugs it to her.

'Where did you get that?' I ask.

'Yomjima made it for me.' She points to a woman sitting in the shade of a proper tent. She's looking our way and I give her a wave.

'That's a lovely doll, Nyanbuot. And it was really nice of her to make it for you.'

Nyanbuot stares at her doll with a loving look while I go over to Yomjima to thank her.

She smiles at me with kind eyes. 'Juba, your sister reminds me of my daughter,' she says, and my heart bleeds. I know that Nyanbuot and Mama helped Yomjima bury her daughter along the way to the camp. And that Yomjima helped bury Thon when it was his time.

'Nyanbuot, though, she is strong,' says Yomjima. 'Brave, even though she's still a little girl. And I'm happy to do something for her. I have no family of my own left. The war has stolen them all from me.'

She looks at me gently. 'You too, Juba. I know you're also brave. And you're a strong young man. Your mama always sang your praises to me on the way to this place. She knew in her heart you were still alive and that she would be reunited with you. That's what kept her going, especially after Thon died.'

My shoulders straighten when she says this. I want to be a man. I want to be ready for whatever that brings.

But first I want Mama returned to herself.

2

A month or so after our arrival, the UN supplies still haven't arrived. It seems no one was prepared for this number of people in the camp. With each passing day here the hope on even Thiko's face has lessened, bit by bit. We have been safe here in this camp, and that is much to be thankful for, but I can see the hunger on her face and the worry in her eyes.

Some days she and I go together in search of food. This morning I take her hand as we slip through the fence and we walk deep into the jungle, where sunlight filters through the canopy and makes everything glow. It would be better to stay out here, I think, than in the camp, but Mama isn't capable of leaving.

Thiko and I dream of finding small game but we'll be happy with anything edible, fruit, berries, roots. We find very little. We have been walking dejectedly for some time when we hear a buzzing noise. It sounds like flies over a carcass, but when we look we find to our shock not the body of a dead animal, but of a boy about my own size. Marching ants and a cloud of flies crawl over him. Maggots wriggle in and out. His arms and legs are rail-thin but his belly is huge.

The stench hits my nostrils. It's worse than all the bad smells in the camp put together. A putrid, stomach-curdling smell that makes bile lurch up the back of my throat. But there's no food in my stomach to throw up. Thiko whimpers in horror and moves away but I can't take my eyes off him, even though I badly want to. His own eyes are wide open and staring. I think of the hunger that was eating away at his flesh before the flies did, and I wonder how long it will be before it eats mine.

At last I turn away. I grab Thiko and we flee.

'I'm not hungry anymore,' she says quietly when we finally slow down.

'Me either.' Thinking about starving to death has given me a headache. I want to get out of here. Out of this jungle, out of this camp. I want to get all of us back home to Pacong, the way it was. Before the bombing, before the soldiers. It's knowing that things can never go back to how they were that's hardest of all to bear.

To think how hard we longed to reach this camp while we were walking here. Only to discover more suffering. Sometimes I'm not sure where I'd rather be, here in the camp or back on the path, with all its dangers.

Between the tree tops the sky is adrift in a violet haze, like it might rain, but the air is dry. Thiko and I don't talk. I wonder where she's going in her mind. Maybe she's also thinking about Pacong, and its thatch-roofed huts. Maybe she's seeing the maize fields and the wispy golden elephant grass on the plains.

I can't stop thinking about that dead boy. Did he come out here because he knew he was dying or because he hoped to find food that would keep him alive?

When we sit down to rest against a tree trunk, Thiko puts her head on my shoulder. A gentle wind whistles through the branches, rustling leaves, lulling us towards sleep. My eyelids are feeling heavy when the air around us suddenly grows thick. Nothing obvious has changed but something is there that wasn't a few moments ago.

Then comes a rumbling noise.

I nudge Thiko and she jerks up sharply. 'What?' she says. 'What is it?'

But there's nothing to see. I can't figure out where the sound is coming from, or what it could be. It sounds a bit like the feet of a thousand wildebeest running across the savanna, except the ground isn't vibrating.

I grab Thiko's hand and pull her up. 'Come on, we have to get back to camp.' All I can think of is Mama asleep on her reed mat and Nyanbuot keeping watch over her.

As we race through the jungle it strikes me that here we are again, on the run. The rumbling is louder and closer now. Is it a plane? A bomber? The canopy blocks all but little pieces of sky. Would the Sudanese government attack a refugee camp? If they have no problem bombing schools, they could bomb anything, I think.

When the rumbling becomes a roar that sounds like the wrath of God bearing down upon us, I know for certain that there are planes, even though I can't see them. What is happening back in the camp?

And then suddenly, when we're almost out of the jungle, there's silence. But only for a moment. It's interrupted by a whistling sound. I push Thiko down beside the base of a tree, shielding her as best I can. Her face is pressed against my chest and my mind reels as I wait for the moment of impact. Her fingers dig into me. It feels like time has stopped. The whistling continues, but there's no explosion.

At last I open my eyes.

'We're alive,' Thiko says, raising her head.

Then it comes, a *thud*. Followed by another, and another. And more. But still there are no explosions. The sound of the engine is fading and the whistling has ceased but we stay huddled under the tree. At last Thiko gets up and pulls me up after her and we start walking back to the camp.

As we draw nearer, there are voices, people shouting and singing songs. I strain to listen. It's a happy song, a song about food.

'The plane from the UN!' I exclaim to Thiko. I've heard rumours of a plane coming. 'Dropping off supplies. Come on, quickly now.'

We run past the camp boundary to an open field where the grass is shorter. It's littered with blue bags and a stampede is rushing for them. UN workers are shouting orders to get in line but no one takes any notice. People are pushing and screaming and clawing at each other, trying to rip things out of each other's hands. I stare at those food bags and I desperately want one, but I think

I'd be crushed before I could get to it. Thiko and I hover on the edges of the throng, waiting for a chance.

'There's plenty for everyone!' shouts a worker standing nearby, a young woman with long golden hair that shines like silk. She moves with the vigour of someone who's had a good night's sleep and a proper meal. 'Get in line!' she shouts. 'You all have to make a line!'

No one listens. When the woman goes forward she becomes trapped in the throng. She turns and tries to squeeze her way out but the crowd is too thick, they shove her aside. She's going to fall. Someone bumps into her and she bounces into someone else and that stops her from falling. A man pushes in and I think he's going to help her get out but he pushes right over her. She falls on her knees. No one stops to help her. Everyone just wants to get a bag. A woman who has one drops it as she escapes the crush and it splits open when it hits the ground. People swarm on the contents, devouring them right off the dirt like a pack of snarling hyenas.

Thiko grips my hand. I hope Mama and Nyanbuot aren't in this horde. People are yelling and kicking each other, pulling hair, attacking anyone with a bag. I know if I managed to grab something and run, no one could catch me, but I'm afraid Thiko and I would get separated.

We keep to the outer edges as people continue to fight. I see a man punch a woman in the face and take her bag as she collapses. Others trample over her to get to the man, to steal what he has stolen. Corn and beans and sorghum lie everywhere, the bags ripped to shreds. The sweet scent of the corn makes my stomach rumble unbearably.

In the scuffle a small bag has ended up nearby. No one else has noticed. I won't have to leave Thiko on her own for long if I go after it. So I run for it, but just before I get there an older man snatches it. He backhands me as he runs off. I hit the ground hard and he doesn't look back.

Then Thiko is there, helping me up. 'This is madness!' she cries. 'Look at that man over there.' She points to a large man standing guard over two bags, wielding a stick that he swings at anyone who comes close.

And then I see a little boy crawling through the crowd, weaving his way in and out of the churning legs. How did he get there? He must be one of the 'lost boys', with no parents, because no mother or father would let their child near this field. Above him, two women are wrestling over a bag. It falls and lands right in front of him. He dives on top of it but before he can get up, the bag is yanked out from under him. He hangs on as a man lifts the bag up, taking him with it, shaking the bag violently until the boy goes flying off.

I can't believe what I'm seeing. It's like a battlefield. The UN workers have retreated, powerless to do anything as the fighting goes on. And the trampling and the screaming and the snatching from others.

Eventually, when all the bags are gone, the crowd disperses. Thiko and I, along with some others who have stayed out of the fray, go in search of any spillage that might have been missed. We brush the ants off a few kernels of corn and eat them.

The field smells like blood. We come across a couple of dead bodies. One is a woman curled in the dirt, face bloodied. Her arms are cradled close to her, holding something. It feels wrong but I tug it free. It's a gourd and inside is corn. Thiko and I eat a few pieces and then I hide the gourd under my shirt and we head back to camp.

Two men come walking towards us. One of them is Dinka, I can see the tribal marks on his forehead. He's tall, with thin legs like a bird, and he walks with a commanding stride. I can tell his friend is not Dinka, his skin is too light, and as he gets closer I see his oversized red eyes, like a possum's. They're full of pain and trauma, and his face is caked in dirt. They're not carrying anything. Maybe they were looking for food in the jungle and missed the food fight.

I tell Thiko to walk in another direction, away from the men.

'Hey,' the Dinka man calls out. 'Hold on there.'

I grip the gourd tightly and we continue on, but they catch us up and walk along with us a little way. Then the second man says, 'What's that under your shirt?' His voice is calm and he's smiling but my stomach drops.

'Nothing,' I say.

'It's not nothing. You wouldn't be hiding it if it was nothing. Let me see it.'

'No.'

His friend smirks. 'Come on now, we just want to see what you have. There's no harm in letting us see, is there?'

'We have to get back,' I say. 'We're in a bit of a hurry.'

'Give it here.' The Dinka man grabs my arms and pulls them apart and the other man takes the gourd from under my shirt.

'Give it back!' I scream. 'That's ours!'

'Not anymore. Now it's ours.'

I try to grab it back but the possum-eyed man knocks me to the ground like I'm no bigger than a gnat. When I try to scramble up Thiko sits on top of me and won't let me up.

'They're stealing our corn!' I shriek, struggling against her.

'Let them go,' she says. 'It's not worth it. There wasn't much in there anyway.'

Frustration bubbles inside me. I cry and hate myself for it but I can't stop. The only thing I hate more is that Thiko is here to see it. She moves off me and rubs my arm, like Mama does. I sit up and she leans her head on my shoulder.

I wipe at my eyes as I watch the men walk away. Back in Pacong, a grown man, a Dinka man with tribal marks, would never steal, especially not from a girl or a boy. But this man's pride seems to have departed him. I remind myself that this is not Pacong. There's no pride here in this camp. Pride is gone and buried. Now it's only about survival.

Once the men are some distance away, Thiko says, 'Let's go.'

The sun is hanging low, beaming red as fire as we make our way through the camp, past children playing in the dirt who thankfully know nothing of what we've just seen.

When we reach our area, we discover that the day hasn't been all bad, because in place of our shelter is a tent. A proper tent! The light in my heart that went out in the food drop rekindles a little. The tent is big enough to accommodate more than ten people, although we've been given only three blankets.

But Mama isn't there. Nyanbuot says she went to look for me. 'She heard shouting and was worried. I'm not supposed to leave the tent. I've been sitting here on my mat.'

By the time Mama returns, the sun has long been down. I jump up when she pushes the tent flaps aside.

'Where were you?' she says immediately, rushing over to hug me. 'Why didn't you come back?'

'I went to look for food from the plane drop. But it was madness, Mama. Everyone just went crazy. I wasn't able to get anything.'

'At least you're unharmed,' she says. 'I thought you'd been trampled. I looked everywhere.'

'I nearly had food,' I say. 'But someone took it off me.'

Mama shakes her head. 'Well, we mustn't dwell on what is gone. It will only make the hunger worse. God will bring us something if we're patient.'

And I want to believe her, I do, but after that terrible fight I don't know if I can. I'm not even sure God is still in this country. If he still remembers us. But at least we have a tent now, protection from the weather, and that's enough to bring my hope back. Thiko and her mother, I discover, have been given a tent not far from ours.

That night, Yomjima comes to see us. She has a cloth in her hand, folded around something.

'This is for the three of you,' she whispers to Mama and Nyanbuot and me. She unwraps the cloth and lying there are cooked corn grains and little cups of something pale.

We just stare at her and she says, 'Go ahead, I already ate. I saved this for you.'

Our thanks seem inadequate but we eat. The pale stuff in the cups is applesauce, which I've only tasted once before, when a neighbour in Pacong was sent some by a relative. It's sweet and soothing on my throat. I lick my fingers for every last trace.

When we're done, Mama takes Yomjima's hand. 'Yomjima . . . I don't know how to thank you.'

'Shh,' she says, 'don't you be silly. You'd have done the same for me.' Her face turns solemn. 'It was terrible out there.'

Mama looks at me. 'Juba and Thiko were there. He told me what happened. I don't want to believe it.'

'You should sleep in our tent tonight,' Mama tells her. 'Please. Stay with us.'

Yomjima agrees and goes to get her mat. She and Mama talk and giggle like schoolgirls until it's late, and from that night on Yomjima becomes part of our family. She brings Mama back to the way she used to be. Soon Nyanbuot and I are calling her Aunt Yomjima, and I can tell by the big smile on her face every time we say it how happy it makes her.

The day after the fights, Yomjima shares more of her food with us. I save a cup of applesauce for Thiko, whose eyes widen when I take it to her.

'Juba! Where did you get this?'

'From Yomjima. But now it's for you.'

She beams and eats it up and the whole day feels fresher now that we have food in our bellies.

A little later, Chieng comes by with Majok and Majok's cousin Makol, a thin boy with chubby cheeks. They too now sleep in a proper tent, all three in the same one. None of them had gone to the food drop.

'If I had been there,' Chieng says, 'I would've grabbed the biggest bag I could and ran.' He swings his arms wildly in the air.

I don't want to tell him what would have happened to him if that mob had caught him with his bag of food. Instead, to change the subject, I start telling a story of Grandpa's and soon I have an audience. Children and older boys gather round, some my friends, some I don't know, some of them lost boys. I tell a tale about a fox, a snake and a leopard. I keep my voice animated and use a different one for each character, making quick movements for the fox, a slow weaving for the snake, a deep crouching for the leopard. I like feeling everyone's eyes on me, knowing they're listening to every word. When I finish the last story, we all have smiles on our faces.

That was a good day.

Whenever a new group of refugees arrives in the camp, Chieng and I go to see if any of his family are among them. We ask the UN people first, then the Red Cross, then we go from group to group. By now I'm really only trying to be a good friend to Chieng by going with him. I don't have much hope that he will find anyone from his family.

But Chieng's hopes and energy are still high as we shake people's hands, asking over and over if they have news. Every time, we get a negative answer, but still Chieng remains hopeful. He believes his mother and the others are alive. Sometimes I think it might be better to end the search, but I know I can't ask him to give up.

Mama is unwell. She's fallen back to her old ways of sleeping for long stretches and staring at the ground when she isn't asleep. Not even Yomjima can get her to snap out of it.

'Your mama has been through a lot,' Yomjima tells me. 'Too much for one person to go through.'

But Yomjima has been through just as much, I think to myself, and besides, it's more than that. Mama has a deep, hacking cough. She spits blood and then tries to hide it from us, but we've seen it. She's constantly shivering. I gather all the blankets we have and cover her. I fear she has the wasting disease.

When I ask her how she's feeling, she pats the ground next to her mat. 'Sit with me for a few minutes, Juba. Keep your old mama company.'

I sit, smiling. 'You're far from old, Mama.'

This almost gets a laugh out of her, though I'm afraid it's for the wrong reason. She squeezes my hand. 'You're a sweet boy,' she says.

I see how dry and cracked her lips are, how pale she looks, the tiredness in her eyes. I fill our plastic cup from the jerry can and hold it to her mouth. 'You need to drink something,' I say.

She takes a tiny sip and immediately starts hacking. Wiping the spittle from her lips she looks over at Nyanbuot, who is cleaning debris from the dirt floor a few feet away. Mama pulls me closer and says in a low voice, 'Your sister looks up to you,' she whispers. 'No matter what happens, you must protect her with your life.'

The way she's talking makes it sound like she's asking me to watch out for Nyanbuot because she won't be around to do it.

'Mama,' I begin.

'Shh. You must be strong. You must watch out for your sister. Promise me that.'

'Of course, Mama. You don't even have to ask.'

She nods. 'Thank you, son. That's all I wanted to hear. Thank the Lord we are still alive and together,' she says. She raises her arm weakly and rubs my back, but she continues to shiver despite the blankets. I don't know how to help her. I don't know what to do.

I tell Nyanbuot to stay with her and I run to the clinic nearest to us, at the southern end of the camp. I know there's another clinic at the northern end, and I've heard that each one has two doctors and five nurses. So I'm hopeful that one of them will be able to help.

But when I arrive, there's a long line outside. The clinic is in a large tent with a sign on it saying 'Doctors Without Borders'. I join the line and tap my fingers against my thighs impatiently, my mind full of worry about my mother. When I finally reach the desk at the front of the tent, I describe her condition to the nurse, a pretty woman with a giant smile. Behind her I can see partitions dividing the tent into rooms. The nurse tells me Mama needs medicine, but they're out of it just now because so many people are sick. They will get more, she says, but she doesn't know when. She offers me bandages. I don't know what I can do with bandages but I take them anyway. I wonder why the planes didn't bring medicines in with the food.

I stay by Mama's side late into the night, even after she and Nyanbuot have gone to sleep. Yomjima's mat is empty. I don't know where she is. She's slept here every night since she first came to us with the applesauce and corn.

Lying next to Mama I stare up at the roof of the tent, wishing I could see the sky, the stars. My eyes feel heavy but I'm afraid if I go to sleep Mama will wake up and need me. I don't want her to lie there awake alone.

After four days she says she feels better. So it wasn't the wasting disease. This is cause for great thanks. But Yomjima still hasn't returned, and she isn't in her old tent either. I've missed her kindness, and her help.

No sooner is Mama on the mend than I hear Nyanbuot crying in her sleep. This happens two nights in a row, and when I hear her crying on the second night I get up and crawl over to her.

I nudge her but she doesn't stir, or stop crying. I pull her arm and she jumps awake.

'What?' she says in alarm.

'Shh. You were crying in your sleep,' I whisper. She puts her hands to her face and discovers I'm telling the truth. I snuggle up close and wipe away her tears.

'Were you dreaming about bad things?' I ask, and she nods. 'You know, I have bad dreams sometimes too, but it doesn't mean they'll come true. Try not to worry about them.'

'The only time I feel happy in my dreams is when I'm playing with Thon.'

Hearing my brother's name makes my stomach knot. 'Me too,' I say, and we lie silently for a few moments.

'He will always be in our hearts,' I tell Nyanbuot.

'I wish I could play with him again.'

'I know. So do I.'

'I wish I could see him smile.'

Now the tears are flowing down my own face but I don't want Nyanbuot to know.

'It's not fair,' she says. 'Why did those men have to do those things?'

I put a hand on her cheek. I remember when I used to carry Thon on my back to the river, how he'd never want to get down when we reached the water. I think of the times he did his crazy dance moves in the compound and Mama laughed and clapped. My father would join the dancing. And with eyes that were never dull, eyes that shined bright as the sunrise over the Nile, Mama sang for them. Like a songbird. Sometimes the other men of Pacong would look at my father and shake their heads. Men weren't supposed to laugh with their wives all the time, but that was Dad. That was our family.

Out beyond the confines of this tent, the wind plays the same song repeatedly, whistling in the trees. Eventually Nyanbuot falls back asleep, but I stay awake. And then I hear shrieking. It's away in the distance but it's a sound I know, I've heard it all my life.

Rats.

I get up quietly and go outside, grabbing a stick. I follow the sound and come upon two rats fighting. They're entangled in each other and aren't aware of me. I stab one in the head with the sharp end of the stick, stepping on the other's tail when it tries to scamper off. When the first rat is dead, I stab the other one. I remember how I used to fear rats. In the village they were pests that could bite and make us sick. Here they are food.

It's still early as I'm roasting the rats over a little fire behind our tent, hoping the smell won't attract too much attention, but soon enough I hear footsteps approaching. I place myself in front of the rats and a boy appears, his nose up, sniffing the air like a dog.

'I smell steak,' he says, inhaling deeply. 'It smells good. Do you smell it?'

I widen my eyes and sniff the air too. 'No. I wish I could. I'd give anything to smell steak. But I think your nose is playing tricks on you, because you're hungry.'

The boy blinks. 'No, I *can* smell it.'

'You're imagining it,' I laugh. 'You must be smelling the steak you had some time ago in your village. It's a cruel trick of your mind.'

'Your mind can do that to you?' he asks incredulously.

'The mind can play all sorts of tricks on you,' I say. 'It can be enough to drive you mad.'

He looks horrified. 'I can't believe it. I don't want to smell something that isn't there!' He runs off and I breathe a sigh of relief, even as my heart whispers its guilt for lying to the boy.

Once I'm sure he's not coming back, I rouse Mama and Nyanbuot and we sneak away to the cover of the bushes to eat our feast. It's been so long since I had meat and it tastes like the best meat I've ever eaten.

Mama licks her fingers for every last piece. 'God always provides,' she says, and I have no trouble believing her now. I silently thank him for letting me hear the rats in the night, and I can't help feeling like a true provider.

'Should we save some for Yomjima?' I ask, even though we haven't seen her in days, and Mama looks sad again. 'I don't think so,' she says. But I set some aside for Thiko, although two rats provide little meat.

Nyanbuot hugs me, her fingers slick with grease. I pull Mama to her feet and she leans against me as we walk back, our bellies sated. I'm surprised to realise that I can now see over her shoulder; I'm only a few inches shorter than her. I can see the top of her head if I stand on my toes. When did that happen? Despite everything, I've still been able to grow.

Nyanbuot skips ahead of us, circles back and then runs ahead again. The sun is warm and the sky is the cloudless blue I know well. A good morning becomes a good day when I give Thiko her rat meat and in return she gives me a kiss on the cheek.

3

One day, something happens in the camp that changes everything for me and the other boys around me.

Spirits had been lagging, we were all wishing harder than ever to be somewhere else. People bickered and argued about everything, if for no other reason than to have something to do, to take their mind off being here, being hungry. The priest from Pacong would walk past and give no response when I said hello. I didn't know what had happened to him. Maybe he no longer recognised me. Whenever I greeted him in our village, he always responded with 'God bless you.'

I remembered him standing in the church after our school

was bombed, holding his wooden cross high, and with the Great Spirit in his voice as he told the congregation not to surrender to the work of evil. He organised prayers and home visits for the wounded. He had been tall and unbending, like a pole. Now he looked defeated.

The worst day was when we learnt that a peacekeeping soldier had discovered Yomjima's body hanging from a tree, a mile or so outside the compound. There was a burial and Mama said a few words, forcing herself not to cry.

No one said it, but I couldn't get rid of the feeling that Yomjima did this to herself. She was happy about sharing our tent but I knew she never stopped thinking about her family and everyone she'd lost. Yomjima was so kind to us and she kept Mama strong, she even claimed that it was Mama who had suffered too much. I never suspected that beneath her hopeful manner she had already lost hope herself. And I couldn't stop wondering if there was something we could have done to save her. Everything felt so dark.

Nyanbuot was more upset than anyone. Afterwards she would not let the stick doll Yomjima gave her out of her sight.

The day that things change begins with me going to the jungle to forage. On my way back I see a group of boys playing in the field where the food drop happened, and as I get closer, I see that they're chasing something. It's hard to tell what, because there are so many legs and feet moving in different directions.

'Kick it, kick it!' the boys yell and shout.

It's a game of football! I discover that they're using balled-up plastic bags, all stuffed inside each other and then inside one larger bag. It doesn't matter how hard anyone kicks it, it never goes far, but none of the boys care about that. Some old buckets have been set as goal markers at either end of the field.

Chieng and Majok are right there in the thick of things, and when they see me they grin madly.

'Juba!' Chieng calls. 'Come and play football!' His face is covered in sweat and dirt. I haven't seen him look so happy in ages.

'Yes, come and join us!' Majok yells. The ball of plastic bags whizzes by him and he's after it in a flash. Then he runs over and says he and Chieng came looking for me when they heard about the football, but couldn't find me.

I need no more encouragement. I sprint out to join them and am quickly one of the group. There are about twenty-five or so of us, not in teams, just a frenzy of kicking and pushing and giggling and raucous shouting.

'Don't let *him* get it!' one boy yells, but in a good-natured way. The group changes direction as one and we run to the opposite end of the field, laughing helplessly at how uncontrollable the ball of plastic bags is. I forget my hunger. My sadness and frustration drop away. And going by the faces of the others, they feel the same. I can't believe no one thought of this before.

We play until the light has gone, and next day we're all back on the field to play again. And then again the next day. I'm not sure who notices him first, but one day we realise that a man is watching us. He's standing at the edge of our game, a tall and lanky white man with light flowing hair. He looks like he's in his twenties but it's hard to tell.

It's Majok who eventually stops the game and goes over to ask the man if he wants to join in. We all follow.

'No, no,' he says, 'I'm just enjoying watching. Even if you guys are doing it all wrong.' He laughs when he says this, so no one will be offended.

'Well, it's not like we're professional footballers,' Chieng says. 'We're just having fun.'

We did play a kind of football back in Pacong, those of us from that village, but we don't know the proper techniques of the game. None of the other boys in this group seem to either. I wonder how we'd be able to play properly anyway, with our ball of plastic bags.

'And it's great that you're having fun,' the man says. 'But would you like to learn how to play properly? Rather than chasing around a . . . What is that thing, anyway?' He nods to our makeshift ball.

'It's plastic bags,' someone says.

'Who are you?' another boy asks. 'Why don't you leave us alone if you're only going to criticise what we're doing?'

'I'm not criticising,' the guy says, holding up his hands. 'I admire you boys for doing something like this here. But if you'd like, I could give you a few pointers. I happen to know a thing or two about football.'

It seems too good to be true. We all look at each other. That an adult, a white man, is showing interest in us is surprising enough, and that he wants to help us is even more surprising. But we've all silently agreed we want his help.

At last Majok says, 'Okay,' and the man extends his hand.

'My name's Philip,' he says.

'Did you used to play for a team?' I ask.

'I did, before I became a volunteer. My main position was attacking midfielder, although I was also a pretty good centre forward, which is the most celebrated position in football. But I loved playing as a midfielder best.' He tells us that the organisation he's with runs recreation programs for refugees. He's only just come to our camp after working in others, and hasn't found people interested in football until now.

We're all silently impressed by his experience, and a bit shy. Then he asks us for our names, and whether any of us have ever played a proper game of football, with two full teams. None of us have.

'Well,' says Philip, 'we can change that. I'll give you some training drills and later we can make up teams.' He casts an eye over the group of us. 'There are enough of you to make two teams. Then eventually you can have a real game.' He chuckles. 'We've sure got the time.'

'Great,' says Chieng. 'What do we do first?'

'First you're going to need a better ball,' Philip says. 'A real ball would be ideal but . . .' His voice trails off but we don't need to be told what the chances of a real ball are.

'Where are we going to find something better?' asks one of the boys. 'Can you make us something?'

Philip looks amused. 'How about you go for a bit of a hunt and see what you can find,' he says. 'Hopefully something a little more solid than plastic bags.'

We all scatter, eager to be the one to come across the makings of a good football. As I search for something that might work, I think about how much Deng would like being among this group. Maybe if I learn to play properly I can teach him too, when I finally see him again. Maybe we can teach everyone from our village. And for a moment, the refugee camp transforms into Pacong and

I imagine that all my friends and family, all our neighbours, are together the way we used to be.

When we regroup we discover that someone has found old cardboard. We compact this and then take apart our ball of plastic bags and remake it with the cardboard inside. It's still nothing like a real ball but it has more weight than the bags alone, and there's more chance of it going where you intend it to when you kick it. Philip shows us the correct techniques for kicking and gives us some drills and we spend the rest of the afternoon practising.

Majok, unused to the new technique, goes to kick the ball and misses it entirely. His foot lands on another boy's knee, causing him to fall. The boy immediately gets up and charges at Majok. Once Philip has broken them up he warns us all that fighting is not allowed on the football field.

When Chieng asks about forming teams, Philip says, 'We're not ready for that yet. For now, you still need to practise, so you really understand the techniques and the game. But I can see that you're all fast learners, you've made a lot of progress today already. You should be proud of yourselves.'

'Will you be here tomorrow?' Majok asks.

'Yes, but even if I'm not out here, you can still practise. Practise whenever you can, and in no time you'll be able to play your first match.'

When I tell Mama and Nyanbuot about Philip and how we'll be learning to play football properly, it makes Mama nearly as happy as it's made me.

'It's so wonderful you boys have that to do,' she says.

'Can we come and watch?' Nyanbuot asks.

'Of course,' I say, 'when we play a real match.'

I have no idea when that might be. And what if Philip never shows up again? But for now I feel happy. Here in this place it's important to be reminded that you still know how to be happy.

I needn't have worried about Philip not showing up, because he's there the next day. All the boys from yesterday are here, as well as others who've heard about it. We make extra balls out of the cardboard and plastic bags, and Philip breaks us up into groups to do drills. Then he explains all the rules of the game in great detail, and has to answer a lot of questions about them. After that he asks who's interested in being goalkeeper and he shows those boys how to block the ball and how to anticipate where a player will try to get a shot in.

We play in peace, even if we sometimes unintentionally kick each other instead of the ball. I am not the best player, not by a long way, but no one is keeping track of who's better. Except maybe Chieng, who's always competitive. Chieng always wants to be the best.

'Is that as far as you can kick the ball, Juba?' he taunts. 'Watch this.'

He takes an elaborate run-up and kicks, but the ball doesn't even go as far as the one I've just kicked. I try not to smile.

'The wind knocked it down,' he says. 'Let me try that again.'

Bol is among the boys who joined us today and he strolls over and stands next to me. Even though he's remained friendly since I arrived at the camp, I still can't help feeling wary. Maybe he has some plan to lull me into letting my guard down.

'It's funny,' he says, 'I was remembering that conversation we had back in Pacong, when I told you to pick any game and I'd beat you at it. That feels like a long time ago now, doesn't it?'

'Yes,' I say. It's hard to tell whether he's feeling happy or aggressive.

'Well, I think Majok is the only player here better than me at football,' he declares.

It's true, Majok plays well, as if it's something he's always done. Even Philip is impressed, and I overhear him telling Majok that he'll make a good footballer.

Majok beams. 'Maybe I can play on your team when we finally get out of here.'

'I think you'd have a strong chance at something like that,' Philip says.

'*If* we ever get out of here,' another boy adds.

I'm happy for Majok but I'm bothered by that last comment. Surely we won't be staying here forever. This isn't home, it's a temporary resting place, where we'll wait out the conflict. We might not be able to go back to Pacong, but there'll be somewhere new to start over. This camp is not our new beginning.

A week goes by before Philip announces it's time to pick the teams. Majok is made captain of one team and Chieng is captain of the other. Everyone can see that Majok should be a captain because he's naturally good at the game, but I'm not sure why Philip has chosen Chieng. He's not bad at football but he's not as good as someone like Bol, and he doesn't need the ego boost.

With the two captains decided on, Philip has the rest of us stand in a group and then splits us in half.

'This side, you're on Majok's team,' he says. 'And this, you're on Chieng's.'

I'm standing right in the middle, which means I can easily slip onto either team. I choose Majok's. Bol, I see, is on Chieng's. There are enough of us for each team to have substitutes as well.

'I've told you guys before how impressed I am with the effort you've put into this,' Philip says, 'and you've all improved enormously, much quicker than I'd have thought. You've been working hard. So now that we have our teams we can play a practice game.'

'How will we know who's on which team?' Chieng asks. 'We don't have jerseys.'

'Not yet you don't,' Philip says, in such a way that it's easy to imagine there are jerseys on their way to us, from somewhere. We know that can't be true but it's fun to think of. 'In the meantime, your team, Chieng, will play without shirts, and be the Skins. Majok's team will keep their shirts on and be the Shirts.'

The boys on Chieng's team eagerly pull off their shirts and toss them in a careless pile, not bothered about how they will sort them out later. For the rest of the afternoon we play a scrappy game without keeping score. Philip umpires minimally, just enough to keep things flowing.

'Great,' he says at the end of the day. 'You've all shown that you can play as a team member and you understand the game. I think we can have a real game in a few weeks. Do you guys feel up for that challenge? Do you want to play a game for your families and friends to watch?'

There's a resounding *yes* and a noticeable buzz of excitement. But for now, it's still practice, practice and more practice.

That night, my muscles ache as I lie on my mat but I'm feeling grateful and happy. Sleep must have come quickly because I don't remember closing my eyes and then suddenly I'm jolted awake. There's a noise outside, one that seems familiar. People are stirring around me, whispering.

'Why would they be dropping food now?' I hear someone say, and I realise the noise is a plane.

'Who cares?' another responds. 'They can drop food any time they like!'

A murmur of agreement runs through the tent. People get up and move out into the night. I follow with Mama and Nyanbuot. The rain of the early evening has let up and the air is fresh and clean.

'There it is!' someone shouts. Others have come from neighbouring tents to see what's happening.

People cheer. But underneath that I can hear yelling, and it doesn't sound happy or excited. Someone is yelling, 'That isn't a UN plane!'

The plane is so close now I can hear nothing else. And then things are falling from it.

Not food.

Oh no, please, not again.

People scream and peel away or drop to the ground. I grab Mama and Nyanbuot and pull them back to our tent, even though a tent will be no protection against bombs. For some reason I'm remembering the time Nathan paid for us to watch Oprah at the TV shop in Pacong. I wonder if the bombers watch the Oprah show, and if there's a way she can tell them how to behave so they'll leave us alone. So they'll stop bombing us.

There's an explosion nearby but it's only a small one. The plane careens low over us. Then just as suddenly it disappears.

No one is sure what has just happened.

'The rain kept the bombs from exploding,' someone says.

'We're all very lucky!'

'That was only a warning,' says someone else. 'They'll be coming back. They're going to bomb this whole camp into the ground. We're not safe here.'

Mama pulls me and Nyanbuot close. 'Don't listen to what anyone else is saying. Right now, here is our safest option.'

'But *why* do they want to bomb us?' Nyanbuot asks, and I hate hearing the fear in her voice.

Mama squeezes us both. 'I don't know,' she says. 'I just don't know.'

I wonder if anyone knows the answer to that.

4

Chieng wakes me before sunrise and tells me he dreamt of his family. No new groups of refugees arrived in the night, after the plane flew over, and it seems pointless to go in search, but I go with him anyway, to the edge of the camp where no tents have been set up as yet and the people are still in shelters. Once, we were at the edge of the camp, but it's continued to grow so quickly that the edge is now some distance from us.

But the way the adults are sitting on the ground stops us going to ask them about Chieng's family. They seem as if their spirit has been killed, and I think it must be because of that plane.

There are children, though, who are oblivious to their situation. They crowd round a white woman who is chatting with them and laughing, just like people used to do with Nathan. She hoists the smallest child onto her shoulders and the others redouble their cries for attention.

She heads over to a Landcruiser with a Save the Children logo on the side and they mill about her legs. Three white workers in safety gear are putting up a fence and a warning sign around the bombs that didn't explode last night. One of the workers is the young blond woman I saw the day of the food drop.

I turn around at the sound of another vehicle and see a UN Landcruiser roll up. Two men get out and go to talk with the workers. Now the blond woman starts yelling at the men about something, though she's talking so quickly I can't make out what she's saying. People gather to see what the commotion is about.

I walk a little closer and hear her say, 'People are dying! Women and children and men who have no relatives. And now they're being thrown away without a proper burial, like diseased chickens. Carried into the jungle where wild animals can feed on them. We need more help here and it's just not happening. People will turn on us, they're going to think *we're* the enemy!'

She hits one of the men in the chest with both fists and I'm afraid of what will happen to her now, but then she collapses into his arms sobbing. The man leans down to say something to her, I can't hear what, but eventually he calms her and everyone disperses. Chieng and I head back without having asked a soul about his family.

Later that day, some people are given UN ration cards, but not everyone. My family doesn't get one. None of my friends get one. I can't work out how they decide who gets a card and who doesn't, how it's decided who will eat and who will not. I've discovered from Bol that his father reached the camp just before the big increase in numbers, and that's why he got a ration card.

And then at last food trucks arrive. Another thing I don't know is why it's trucks and not planes this time, but it's still only the people with cards who can get food. I wonder if my family and I will ever be able to get anything.

Mama tries to explain that those in most need are given priority, and some people need to be fed high-energy biscuits. She's heard of one man who was apparently so weak by the time he got his biscuit that he couldn't eat it and had to be taken to the clinic. Mama tells me they can't issue too many cards because there isn't enough food to go round, and people will only fight for a share if they all have a card.

This makes no sense to me. We're here whether they give us cards or not, we're hungry, and it seems unfair that we have to wait until everyone with a card has food before we get anything.

'More cards will arrive soon,' one of the UN workers tells us. 'Those who did not receive one need to be patient and know that more will come. Hang in there!'

Easier said than done, I think as people swarm the food trucks. Nyanbuot and I can only stand and watch as those with cards walk past with cups of sorghum or corn. No one offers to share.

My stomach rumbles. When I go to our makeshift football field for practice that afternoon I find it difficult to keep focused on the drills. Today, Chieng has decided he wants to have a go at being goalkeeper, and Philip has us all line up and try to kick a ball past him.

'No way are you going to get that past me, Juba!' Chieng says when it's my turn. And he's probably right. My head feels light from lack of food.

Chieng is leaning forward, knees slightly bent, a fierce look on his face. He's been calling taunts to everyone, but I feel like he's more determined now that I'm up here. I wonder why, seeing we're friends, but that's the way it's always been between him and me. There's always been an unspoken competitive streak. We're like brothers in this.

I give the ball the best kick I can but Chieng blocks it. He beams and punches the air as if he's the best goalkeeper in the world. I might be more upset if I weren't still thinking about food.

The next day, I'm walking with Nyanbuot to the jungle to forage when we see a long table set up near the centre of the camp. On it are several large cooking pots, and when we come closer we learn that it's porridge.

Nyanbuot and I turn back and join the end of the line. We wait for a long time and when we finally reach the front, we come before the blond woman who was yelling and sobbing the day before. She smiles and asks to see our ration cards.

I look at her, hoping she will understand, and say, 'We're really hungry.'

'I'm sure you are. Show me your card and I'll fill up your bowl.'

'We . . . we don't have cards yet. A man told me we'd be getting them soon.'

The smile on her face falters. 'This food is for those who have cards.'

'But —'

'Get out of the line if you don't have a card!' someone behind us shouts.

My heart sinks. We're not going to be given even a little.

'When will you have cards for my family?' Nyanbuot asks.

'I don't know, dear. Maybe if someone dies you can have their card. Now hurry along, you're holding up the line.'

Nyanbuot runs off crying.

'You shouldn't have said that,' I tell the woman angrily.

She barely glances at me. 'There are hundreds of children in the same situation you're in.'

'We're not hundreds of children,' I say. 'My name is Juba. That's my sister Nyanbuot.'

'Please just let me do my job.' She hasn't stopped her ladling.

I think I hate that woman.

I catch up to Nyanbuot, take her hand and lead her towards the jungle. 'Come on,' I say. 'I bet we can find some berries. Maybe I'll find another rat.'

This brightens her spirits and we spend hours searching. All we find are three mushrooms.

'These look okay,' Mama says when we take them to her. 'Not poisonous. Let's cook them.'

Nyanbuot gets water and Mama boils the mushrooms and we share a tiny bowl of mushroom soup.

Several days later, Chieng, Majok and I are wandering around at the edge of the camp, beyond the tents and shelters. There are few people here. When we hear a loud noise I look over to see that a UN truck has overturned a short way off.

I don't wait for my friends. There might be food on that truck, and if there's any to be salvaged I will make sure that this time my family gets some. I sprint over to find the truck lying on its side at a crazy angle, dangling over a steep ditch. It looks like it could topple right in at any moment.

Then I hear someone screaming for help from the cab of the truck. It sounds like a woman's voice.

The windows are wound up and dusty but I peer in. It's the mean blond woman! Blood is trickling from her nose. She starts when she sees me staring in at her. I recall the words she said to Nyanbuot and consider, for the briefest moment, leaving her here. It would be justice for her and her harsh dismissal of my family's needs. But that won't bring me a ration card any sooner.

'Please help me,' she yells. 'I can't undo the seatbelt and the door is stuck!'

The door is nearly horizontal and the handle is hard to reach. I brace myself and give it a tug but it only opens a few inches. I'm worried that if I tug any harder I'll lose my balance and fall in the ditch myself.

Majok and Chieng are here now and both have a go at opening the door. It shifts a little further. It might be enough for her to slide out, I think, if she can just get her seatbelt off. Carefully I position myself over the door, with one hand on the roof to prop myself up, and I reach my other hand in through the gap, groping for the belt. I get my fingers around it but I can't undo it, and the woman won't sit still. The truck is wobbling dangerously.

'You've got to stop moving!' I shout at her. 'Don't panic!'

She calms a little. Other people have arrived now, and one leaves again immediately to get help. Someone warns me that I'll end up in the ditch with her and the truck if I don't move off it, but I keep tugging on the seatbelt and after what seems like a lifetime it suddenly releases.

The woman shrugs off the belt and repositions herself in the seat so that she can push against the door with her whole body. I move myself out of the way and she forces it open enough to get an arm and a leg out. A group of us manage to haul her out the rest of the way and place her on the ground.

The truck remains where it was, perched over the ditch, and she's still shaking when a UN Landcruiser pulls up. Two men and two women get out, the women with first aid kits. When they've assessed the scene one of the women says, 'I'll tend to her. You take care of the boy's cut.'

Only when she says this do I become aware of a pain in my left arm. The gash is raw and red.

'G'day,' says the second woman as she puts her first aid kit on the ground.

'G'day,' I repeat, although I don't know what she's said. But it sounded like a greeting.

'Can you let me see your arm?'

I hold it out gingerly, then screech as she examines it. 'Ow, that hurts!'

'I'm sure. But you'll be okay.'

'Juba!' Chieng is waving at me frantically, motioning for me to come with him. I glance at the nurse, who is hunting in her kit, head down, then I get up and run over to Chieng. I ignore the calls of the nurse, who is now yelling at me to come back.

Chieng leads me to a cluster of shrubs where Majok is waiting. He looks cautiously over his shoulder, as though fearful of being followed, then drops down on one knee and scratches in the dirt and pulls out a biscuit pack.

I gasp. It's BP-5 Compact Food. I know that these are the biscuits given to weak adults and malnourished children. They can be eaten straight or mixed with water to make a porridge. Trust Chieng to find a way to get hold of them, but right now I'm just glad that he did.

He tears open the package. There are a lot of biscuits, plenty for Thiko, Nyanbuot and Mama as well. We eat our fill and then head back to our tents to share the rest.

We're nearly there when we meet Thiko. 'What happened to you?' she asks, looking at my arm.

'Juba saved a lady,' Chieng says. 'He pulled her from a truck that was about to fall into a ravine.'

'It wasn't really a ravine,' I say.

Thiko's eyes widen. 'You can tell me all about it later,' she says. 'But first, that arm doesn't look good. Come with me.'

I follow her back to her tent, where she wets a piece of cloth with water from the jerry can and cleans my wound. Then she rips another piece of cloth and ties it around my arm. I try not to wince as her fingers secure the fabric.

'That lady was lucky you were there,' she says.

I smile. My arm doesn't hurt any less but I don't think I need to see another nurse for it.

Next morning my arm is throbbing. I unwrap the cloth and leave it off to let the skin breathe for a while. Mama tells me I need to go to the clinic and have it treated properly, and when Thiko comes to check on me she insists we go together. Once we get there we find a line, of course, and we must wait.

Life in the camp is all about waiting. For water, for food, for a ration card, for anything at all. Waiting and wanting. When nothing comes from all this waiting, people swallow mud and pull bark from the trees. Those who eat mud get sick. They vomit, even though there's hardly anything in their stomachs to throw up. They die. This happens all over the camp. I wonder how long it will go on, how much longer people will be able to endure it.

Our football match is the only thing we have to look forward to, but Philip has decided to postpone it because of the events in the camp. Still, I don't let my arm keep me from practice, though I have to be careful. At least it's been properly cleaned and bandaged now.

And then, at last, a familiar sound fills the air and a plane makes another drop. There's a lot more food this time, it seems, and the UN workers are better prepared. After the last drop, Mama heard that no one had been expecting the sudden increase in refugees arriving at the camp, and that was what led to the riot. Now there are peacekeeping soldiers with guns who make everyone stand in line.

But as usual, only the people with ration cards can stand in line, while those of us without hover on the outskirts, hoping that chaos breaks out again, that people will fight and there'll be an opportunity to dash in and snatch something.

The peacekeeping soldiers make sure that doesn't happen. I know it's wrong to wish for disorder, but it's my only chance of getting food. I watch for a while as the lines move slowly, as people shuffle forward, and when I see there really will be nothing for me I turn away.

I'm heading back to our tent when I see the woman from the truck sitting alone on the ground. She looks as though she's not very comfortable. As I walk by she calls, 'Hey!'

I stop and look at her but say nothing.

'Come here,' she says in a kind voice. 'Sit with me.'

I seat myself next to her and she says, 'Are you okay? I haven't even thanked you properly for helping me, so I want to thank you now . . .' She stops and looks a bit embarrassed. 'I know you told me your name but I've forgotten it, I'm sorry.'

I tell her again and she says, 'You're the bravest boy I ever met, Juba.'

I shake my head. 'I'm not brave, Miss.'

'Patricia. And yes you are, you are brave. Not everyone would be prepared to do what you did, not even grown men.'

How can a boy who used to be afraid of rats and snakes be brave? I wonder. But I don't say that. Instead I say, 'Maybe I was just in the right place at the right time.'

She smiles. 'I thought you were going to leave me there. Not that I would've blamed you, the way I spoke to you the other day.'

'I thought about it,' I admit.

She looks closely at me. 'What made you change your mind?'

I shrug. 'I can't remember now.'

'Well,' she says, 'I also want to apologise to you, Juba. For my behaviour at the food line.' Her gaze moves past me to a group of little kids playing in the dirt. 'You know, when I saw the news stories on TV of children with swollen bellies and flies covering their faces, all I wanted was to be able to help. I wanted to make a difference, but . . .'

She stops and takes a deep breath. 'I didn't think it would be easy, but I had no idea it was going to be like this. I honestly didn't think I was going to survive my first day in this camp. I woke up early, but not as early as the people who were already waiting for us to bring them food. It was the dry season then and the dust was horrible, it was swirling everywhere, around everything, like a live thing. It was mocking us. There was no food left in our store. How can you tell starving refugees that there's no food?

'I couldn't sleep my first night here,' she continued. 'I already wanted to go home and I lay on my mat wishing I was somewhere else. I didn't know how I was going to cope here. I couldn't bear the sound of the children crying. I had made a mistake. I should have been back home. I asked myself what the fuck I'd been thinking coming here.'

I flinch at the harsh word. I remember one of my classmates getting into a lot of trouble when he said it in front of Miss Ayen.

'Watch your language, Miss Patricia,' I tell her, and she smiles again.

'Sorry, Juba. But we talk like that in America.'

'Is that where you're from?' I ask.

'Yes. New York City.'

'How long have you been here?'

'Fourteen months.'

That's a long time to be somewhere you don't want to be, I think. I hope I won't be here for that long, but who knows?

'Don't you want to help children anymore?' I say.

'I do, I still do want to help.' She's nodding vigorously. 'But I don't feel like anything I'm doing is helping. I have to wonder what the fu— I mean, what I'm doing here if it's not making a bit of difference.'

'It is making a difference.'

She stares at me. 'How can you say that? Did I make a difference to you? If I did, it was only to make you feel worse. I was cruel to you when I should have been kind, and then you came to my aid.' She looks away again.

After a while she says, 'I miss the sound of my son's laughter.'

'You have a son? Really? How old is he?' I can't imagine how she can be here when she has a son at home.

'Yes. He's back in New York. He's six years old. I spoke with him recently. He wants me to come home. My ex-husband does too. I miss my son so much. I even miss my ex-husband.'

'Then why do you stay?' I know how her boy must be feeling. 'I could barely sleep when I was in the jungle without my mother. A boy needs his mother.'

Patricia looks like she's going to cry. 'Sometimes I think I'll never be able to sleep well again,' she says, as though she didn't hear my question. She looks broken and tired, and I wonder what it must be like to have a family somewhere safe and not be with them. To feel that you have to be here instead.

'I close my eyes and this is all I see.' Patricia gestures around her. 'It's all I hear. No matter how bad things were in my life at home, it was nothing compared to this. Absolutely nothing. This is beyond anything I ever imagined, the suffering.'

I know about wanting to un-see what you've seen. But you can't, and I tell Patricia that. And that she's got to not think about it. 'It'll make you crazy otherwise,' I say, and I wish I had better wisdom to give her. Grandpa would have known what to say.

'I think I'm already crazy,' she says. 'Listen to me – telling you my problems when they're nothing alongside yours and those of your family. I just didn't want you to think I'm as heartless as I might seem.'

'It's the Sudanese government that's crazy,' I say. 'They bomb schools and refugee camps and burn villages.'

She gives a bitter little laugh. 'That's beyond crazy, it's deranged.'

We sit quietly for a few minutes. Then Patricia says, 'Thank you, Juba.'

'You already thanked me,' I say.

'I mean for listening. It helps. You've helped me yet again.'

I stand up and stretch. 'You're welcome,' I say. And I mean it.

5

The day of our football match finally arrives, and while we're all excited I know Chieng is also a little sad. He wants more than anything for his mother to be here to watch him play, but he still has had no news of her. Every time there are new arrivals in the camp, he and I go to see if his mother is among them. Now his hope is running down.

'I think my family is gone, Juba,' he said the last time we headed off to check and came away disappointed yet again, and it took me a long time to answer him. Having someone go missing and not knowing what happened to them is so hard. It leaves a big hole in you that can never be filled.

'She's alive,' I said at last. 'She's somewhere searching for you. You'll find each other.'

We're raising dust now as we walk to the football field, Chieng and Majok and I. My arm has healed well. Bol joins us and declares that his and Chieng's team will win. Chieng agrees wholeheartedly, his competitive nature overcoming his sadness.

'I don't know about that,' Majok says.

'Oh, we will.' Chieng, with his spirits bolstered, is supremely confident, and while I'm happy to see this I wonder if it's genuine or if he's just trying to intimidate me.

'Are you planning to be goalkeeper?' I ask him. 'Because if you are, then I'd say we have a good chance at winning.'

Chieng scoffs good-naturedly. 'What's that supposed to mean? When was the last time you kicked a ball past me? I'm the best goalkeeper in the camp, Juba!'

We reach the field to find that already there are dozens of people gathered in anticipation. My constant hunger and frustration dissipate in the face of these people who've come to watch us. I am part of something, with these other boys, and it will also take these spectators' minds off their daily lives. We'll all be able to lose ourselves in the game. The crowd will get caught up in it and cheer when someone does well, and groan and grit their teeth when a mistake is made.

'This is great,' Majok says under his breath, more to himself than to me or Chieng. His eyes are shining and a smile curves the corners of his mouth.

People keep coming. Thiko and her mother arrive and sit with Nyanbuot and Mama. I wave and they all beam and wave back wildly. I can see Bagic and Koko sitting on an ant mound.

Philip has us warm up, and then I go with Majok's team to one end of the field and Chieng and his team take their shirts off before going to the other end. Philip has chosen the starters for the match and I am a midfielder. I'm the link between the offence and the defence. If I have the opportunity, I can kick a goal.

As we take our places the spectators start to clap, even though we haven't done anything yet. I've never had so many people clap for me before. I smile and wave to the crowd as if I know them all. This must be what it feels like to be famous. Having people who don't even know you looking at you and smiling and clapping. It makes me a bit nervous about failing to perform well in front of them.

Now Philip gestures to a young boy standing at the boundary. The boy runs onto the field holding a bag and Philip opens it and pulls out a ball. A real football!

And it's like when a baby is born in a family. The arrival of something precious. We players grin from cheek to cheek. Some come forward to touch the ball, as if to make sure it's real. Philip has done the impossible and somehow got hold of a proper football. There's no time to ask how before he gets the game under way.

It soon becomes obvious that no one in the crowd has picked a team to go for. They're going for everyone. The ball gets kicked this way, they cheer. It gets intercepted and kicked the other way, they cheer. They're just happy to cheer at anything.

For the first few minutes, I don't even touch the ball. I chase after it but it's always kept in play. Finally I get a chance to kick it to a teammate and manage to do it accurately. I can't believe how differently a real football behaves. As the game goes on

I'm beginning to sweat. We're all playing much harder than we do at practice.

When a player from Chieng's team goes to pass the ball to a teammate I run towards him, and when it rolls in my direction I put a foot out and stop it. I dribble upfield, sidestepping the opposition. They anticipate I'll go one way, I go the other. I'm faster than most boys here. I'm running and dribbling the ball and it's so much easier to do with a real ball. I catch sight of Thiko out of the corner of my eye as I rush past and she's jumping up and down, yelling something I can't make out. I'm trying to get the ball past the attackers waiting to tackle me.

One thing Philip has always stressed is not to try to be a star. If you have the ball, he says, you should look for any teammate in a better position to pass to, not keep the ball and shoot for a goal yourself.

But I'm glancing around and no one is catching me, there's no one coming to intercept the ball. And no teammate ahead of me is in a better position. It feels like the ball and my feet are communicating with each other in a conversation my brain is not part of. The truth is, I only realise later, that if I let my brain get involved, that would mess the whole thing up. I just keep my mind clear. I focus on where I'm going, not on my feet, not on the ball. My feet know where the ball is, the ball knows where my feet are.

Dust swirls around me. Time seems to move slower. I have made it past every opposing player and then I come to Bol. Behind him is Chieng and the goal. Chieng has blocked a few attempts by my team already. If I can kick a goal it will be the first of the game.

I read his body movements. I have to know which direction he will go and I have to deceive him with my own body language, make him think I'll do one thing and then do the opposite. But first I must get past Bol. He looms ahead of me looking like he wants to pound me into the dirt. Any friendliness on his part is gone.

I've slowed to a fast walking speed when he says, 'You can't get that ball past me, Juba.'

Bol is trying to stare me down rather than watching the ball. He's standing with his legs wide, ready to go in whichever direction he thinks I will. I rush forward and kick the ball straight through his legs. It's a short kick and I'm able to sprint by him before he can turn around and I pick up the ball on the other side.

He's behind me now, running to catch up. But I'm not thinking about him because now all that's in front of me is Chieng and the goal. His eyes go from me to the ball and back to my face. He isn't sure where to look. He isn't sure which leg I will kick the ball with. He spreads his arms wide, trying to take up as much space as possible. He's right in the middle of the goal but he's leaning more to the left. I don't know if he realises this, so I make to kick to the left and it's natural for him to continue in that direction. As he does I kick out hard and straight, sending the ball whizzing past his outstretched arms and into the top right corner of the net.

'Goal!' yells Philip.

At first I feel nothing. The moment isn't real. I turn to look at my team, who are in celebration. Majok is running towards me with his arms spread out like he wants to fly. When he reaches me he lifts me up as though I've scored the match-winning goal.

But because it's the first goal it's special and everyone in the crowd is cheering wildly. Chieng is gathering himself up, a bewildered expression on his face. Thiko is laughing madly and waving her arms above her head. Nyanbuot is clapping and Mama removes her hand from her mouth and lets a scream of joy escape. Koko is punching the air and Bagic is doing some crazy dance.

Then suddenly the feelings come and I've never felt prouder or more exhilarated in my whole life. Majok and a teammate hoist me up on their shoulders, the crowd is still roaring and clapping, and even Chieng comes over and grudgingly says, 'Nice shot.' Philip claps me on the back. I don't see Bol.

And it hits me just how strange it is to be in a refugee camp, to be chronically hungry, to not know if you'll ever go home again, and yet to be feeling as if you own half the cows and goats in the world.

I score no more goals that game but my team wins. It doesn't matter, though, who has won and who has lost. For the short while that the match lasted it felt like life was almost normal.

The next morning, Bol seeks me out. I didn't see him at all after the game.

'I've been awake all night,' he says. 'I've been going over it again and again in my mind: how did you manage to slip that ball between my legs? I can't for the life of me figure out how you managed to do that.'

It's hard to read the expression on his face. Is he angry? Is he going to retaliate in some way?

'It was just a lucky chance,' I tell him.

But he grins. 'You're a star for sure,' he says. 'I thought that was going to be my chance to humiliate you,' he confesses. 'I'm bigger than you. I challenged you to a game way back in our village, and yesterday you beat me fair and square. Juba, you have the heart of a lion and the strength of an elephant.'

He holds out a hand to me and I take it. And the exhilaration I feel at there finally being a real truce between us is almost as great as when I scored my goal.

6

The nights grow colder. The paths through the camp have flooded in the rain and the mud has turned sticky as glue. Trucks get stuck in it. More people keep arriving and the UN workers still can't keep up with the demand for tents, so any that the workers think can accommodate more people are given more. That means most of us. It's hard to complain, because no one has anywhere else to go. We're all in this together, and my family was once just like these people, newly arrived with nowhere to sleep. At least the weather hadn't been bad then.

One new boy becomes upset when he tells me about his family, who were shot when their village was attacked. Other people don't want to talk about what happened before they came here, they just stare with empty eyes if you ask. There are two women like this in our tent and one has a young child.

Mama says it's easy for the women in the camp to feel forgotten among all the chaos. She says they've lost their place in the world, along with their homes and possessions and family members and friends. They miss the sense of being part of a community, the easy talking and gossiping they used to enjoy. Here they struggle to create some kind of normality, and sharing a tent is at least a way of feeling safe, part of a pack.

So now I share a sleeping mat with five other boys, with one blanket between us. If you're in the middle it's fine, but whoever gets stuck on the ends winds up freezing. If the other boys fall asleep before me, I steal the blanket and curl myself up under it, but inevitably the coldest boy will wake up and steal the blanket right back. And so it goes all night long.

I long to go and sleep somewhere else, but where? It's even colder outside, and the camp isn't safe at night. I've overheard men talking about the Lord's Resistance Army, saying that the Ugandan rebels have been here in the camp. The LRA have been waging a war since 1987, I learn, and the government of Sudan supports them.

The men say the LRA chose a dark, rainy night to enter the camp. They just walked through the gates with their heads covered and the peacekeeping soldiers took them for one of their units. When the rebels reached the deeper parts of the camp, they went into tents with their guns pointed and warned people not to make any noise. Then they looted their food, clothes and cooking items. They also took two girls and marched away through the back fence into the jungle.

The sleeping situation in Thiko's tent is little better. She too must share a mat with several others.

'One girl cries all night long,' she tells me one morning. We're both tired from our nights of little sleep and from hunger. 'And if you end up next to her, you can feel her shoulders shaking. She doesn't stop. I don't know when she sleeps, because it's certainly not at night.'

'Maybe she's crying in her sleep,' I say. 'Maybe she's the one getting a good night's rest while keeping everyone else awake.' I think about the boy in my tent last night whose farts were almost as loud as his snores.

'The other night I had a dream,' Thiko says. 'We never found this camp. We were still out wandering, you, me and Chieng. Majok too, but not Koko and Bagic. And we weren't scared. We had each other and we knew we'd see our families again, though we didn't know when. Life wasn't that bad. We roamed around, found our own food, we even managed to have fun.' She sighs. 'The football game was great, but apart from that I don't really remember what it's like to have fun anymore.'

Thiko's dream was better than the one I had. I dreamt of running away from huge snakes with long teeth. I'd been out looking for food and was just plucking a ripe mango when one charged me. I screamed until someone woke me up. I didn't tell anybody about that dream and I'm not telling Thiko either, because Momo told me long ago that dreaming of a snake is a sign of bad things to come. I've seen enough bad things already, I don't want to see more. I think instead of the old days back in the village. Like the day Thiko finally conquered her fear and climbed a tree.

I'd told her not to look down until she reached the top, and when she did she perched between the branches, resting her back against the trunk, and closed her eyes and calmed her breathing. Then she gazed out at the scene in front of her. I knew that from up there your eyes could follow the course of the Nile to the southeast, to where the jungle stands on both sides of it, as if giving way to the river.

Thiko looked down at me with a proud grin on her face. 'See?' she said. 'Didn't I say I could climb up here? Am I still a baby now? I've got up to the highest branch.'

'No, you haven't. And I never said you couldn't climb up there. You were afraid to.'

But now that she'd conquered her fear, Thiko was jubilant, and in a mood to taunt. 'Deep down all boys are trembling in fear just like girls,' she said.

'What are you talking about?'

'Have you forgotten that rat the other night?'

How did she know about that? 'I wasn't scared,' I said. 'Or trembling.'

'That's not what your mama told me.'

My mother shouldn't be telling my friends about my fears, I thought. Especially not Thiko. 'Maybe I was a little nervous,' I admitted.

'See, that's what I meant.' She lowered herself from the branch, gripping it in both hands until her feet touched the branch below, and so on until she reached the spot where she had to jump the rest of the way down. Closing her eyes she let go, and fell. 'Ow,' she yelled as she landed hard on her behind.

Meanly, I couldn't help laughing. 'Girls can't jump off trees!'

'I just did!'

She got to her feet and dusted herself off.

'Are you okay?' I asked.

She picked up a stone and threw it at me. 'Don't I look okay?'

I dodged and ran off laughing before she could throw more.

'Yeah, you better run home to your mama,' she called after me.

I stopped then and waited for her, and we held hands as we ran back to the village.

I take her hand again now. I will try to think of something that puts a smile back on her face.

That night, though, is no fun at all. I wake shivering again, curled up in a ball. The other boys on my mat are asleep, the tattered blanket pulled up to their chins. They shouldn't be here, I think. None of us should. This whole place shouldn't exist. We should all still be living in our homes in our villages, going to school, tending our goats and gardens.

I try and fail to get comfortable. The tent is full of snoring and the stale smell of farts. I pull an edge of the blanket over myself and close my eyes but I know I won't be able to fall back asleep. Now there's a baby that won't stop crying. People are stirring and muttering as the mother tries to shush it.

Then she starts singing a lullaby. She sings very softly but she's not far from me and I know the song. Her voice is soothing as I lie awake and listen.

> This world is my home
> It's the air that moves in my breath
> It's the warm breeze that caresses my skin
> I hear the cry of the child born in the time of war

I hear the cry of the children as the elephants fight
Don't cry my child
Even if the elephants fight

Her voice is like a warm breeze itself.

Feel the breeze
See the butterflies
We will all go home, my child
When the elephants stop their fighting.

The woman sings like a caged bird that's only free when it sings. Other people are grumbling now. She has woken them up. But I think I love this woman and her beautiful voice. When the baby quietens she stops singing but I wish her baby would cry again so she would sing more.

In the morning I wake feeling better than I have in days.

Philip has left the camp for a couple of weeks but we continue to practise in his absence. There'll be another match when he returns, he's promised, and he'll even try to bring back uniforms. The thought of this makes us train all the harder.

People say I'm the boy who always makes his shot. And it's true I have a knack for knowing which way an opposing player will move before he moves, so I can then go in the other direction. Chieng is getting better at goalkeeping but it's still easy for me to kick the ball past him, though he blocks the shots of my teammates.

'You're really good, Juba,' Thiko says one day when she comes down to watch us. 'And Chieng isn't doing bad.'

'I think Philip is going to be surprised when he comes back at how much better we've got. Did I tell you he might be bringing us uniforms? Maybe even with our names on them.'

I can't remember if Philip really said that about our names before he left, or if it's just someone's wishful thinking. We'll find out in a few days when Philip is back.

'Then you'll be a real team,' Thiko smiles.

The night before our match I sleep well for once. When I lie down on my crowded mat a scene from the past rolls lazily through my mind. I'm squatting on the riverbank near our home in Pacong. School is finished for the day, the goats have all been fed and returned to the pen, the garden is weeded. Mama is in our hut preparing dinner and Nyanbuot and Thon are up to their ankles in the cool water of the Nile, shading their eyes from the powerful blast of the sinking sun.

'Then what happened, Juba?' Thon asks me eagerly, digging his little toes into the river mud.

'I'll tell you if you can just stop interrupting, Thon.'

He makes a silly face. My brother has been impatient ever since he was a baby wailing for goat milk.

Beside him Nyanbuot waits quietly. She's closed her eyes against the light but I know she's listening carefully.

'Well, the lion had the mouse trapped tight under his huge paw. Even one toe was enough to squash the mouse flat. But before the lion could swallow him down, the mouse said, "Mighty lion, don't eat me. If you spare my life, I will do you a great favour one day." The lion was so taken aback by this that he didn't eat the mouse right off but threw his head back and laughed.'

'Lions don't laugh.' Thon squints up at me from the water. 'Hyenas laugh.'

'It's a story, Thon,' Nyanbuot says. 'Mice don't talk either. But they do in stories. Go on, Juba.'

'So the lion laughed and said, "A mouse? How can a mouse offer a lion any favour? What could you ever do for me?"'

'Juba, Nyanbuot, Thon, dinner!' Grandpa has wandered down from the hut to fetch us.

I leap up from the bank. 'Grandpa's here!'

Nyanbuot runs to him and takes his hand as we head home. Thon pants along beside me on his chubby little legs, wanting to know if the mouse ever did a favour for the lion. I'm just starting to answer him when I hear loud voices. They wake me up.

I am pulled from sleep slowly, my grandfather's voice joining with those from outside. My eyes stay closed but I can no longer see my family or the river. I don't want to be awake. I want to stay on in Pacong.

But I have no choice, the voices quickly turn into angry shouts. There's a thud. Followed by others. It sounds like someone being beaten. The yelling grows louder and I sense that everyone in the tent is awake now, listening. Some people sit up. There is whispering. Then gunfire. Screams. Everyone leaps up at once.

Mama's hand is over Nyanbuot's mouth, who whimpers but does not cry out. Another gunshot pierces the air, closer this time.

I creep to the entrance of the tent and Mama hisses, 'Stay in here, Juba!'

'I just want to have a look,' I say, and I peek out through the flap.

There are LRA rebels everywhere. Too many to count, but there are a lot more of them than there are UN soldiers. As I watch, one of the peacekeepers is shot and falls in a heap to the ground.

I turn around and say, 'LRA!' and gasps run through the tent. People join me at the flap and we watch in horror as the rebels go from tent to tent, yelling orders and dragging women out by the hair, throwing crying children to the ground. The air is full of screaming and sobbing.

'Everyone outside now!' a rebel yells. A few of them appear at the flap of our tent and point their guns at us. 'You too!'

We file out. Mama holds Nyanbuot's hand. A soldier pushes the barrel of his gun into my shoulder to hurry me along. We are all herded over to the football field. I keep looking for more UN soldiers but there are none, although I see Patricia on the field. She has her eyes to the ground, as though she doesn't want to see more suffering. Philip is there too. I haven't seen him since he returned.

Thiko has her arms wrapped around her mother. The singer of lullabies is crying with her baby.

The rebels keep their guns pointed at us as we stand there waiting. I don't know what we're waiting for. Maybe for them to shoot us all? Anger overwhelms me. We're standing here on the football field where we're supposed to be playing our game today.

'Shh,' Thiko whispers, even though I haven't said anything. I know she's saying that because she senses my rage. She doesn't want me to do something stupid and get myself shot. I don't want to get shot either but nor do I want to live like this. What did we do to these men? What right do they have to be here? They are Ugandan rebels and we are South Sudanese refugees. We have nothing in common. I pray that it's only food they want. And then I think how there won't be enough of that to satisfy them in any case.

Now the rebels who've been looting the tents are coming over to the field. Some are wearing football jerseys! They look laughably small on the older men. They all gather and stand around joking with each other. When one of the jersey wearers turns to laugh at something I see my name on his back and it feels like I've been punched in the stomach. I grip Thiko's hand hard. I'm afraid if I let go I'll run right over to that soldier and punch him in the face.

A lot of the rebels are young, some are even younger than me, but they're fierce. They have bloodshot eyes and terrifying stares. I look at a boy wearing a jersey and think how, maybe, in another life, we might have played a friendly football match together, he in his Ugandan team and I in my South Sudanese team, but right now none of them would hesitate to shoot me if they were ordered to. They cradle their guns like precious things, and bullets swing in rows around their necks like beads. But their dark green uniforms are little more than rags, caked with dirt and blood.

The man who is clearly their leader has a patch on his jacket that says 'General Otti' and he carries a stick that looks to be made of ivory. He's an older man with a long scar running from one side of his forehead down across his nose and cheek to the opposite side of his jaw. His face looks like it's been split open and stitched back together.

Now he walks right up to Philip and taps Philip's leg with his stick, as though he's waking him up. I don't know why he's gone to Philip, but maybe it's because Philip looked him in the face.

Then he goes to the lullaby woman, who has sat down with her screaming baby, and yells at them to be quiet. He orders them to get up.

I look away, watch the ants racing across the ground like they're also desperate to be gone from here.

'Please,' says the woman. 'She's hungry. I need to try to feed her, that's all.' When the woman shrieks, I look at them.

Otti has wrenched the baby from her arms. As she lunges after him one of his soldiers springs forward and jerks his rifle up into her face. The general steps back a little way, holding the hysterical baby by one tiny leg with the tips of his fingers. She dangles upside down like a caught rabbit.

The mother is on her knees before the rifles and staring up at Otti, hands clasped in front of her, tears streaming down her face. 'Please, please, please, I beg you, she's only starving. I will keep her quiet. I'll sing her a lullaby. Please, sir.'

He looks from the wet infant to the sobbing mother. 'Obviously you can't keep it quiet,' he says, 'or you would have already.'

'I will do my best, sir. I'll keep her still. Please.'

'Why don't I believe you?' He gives the baby a little shake, and a long, broken gasp passes the woman's lips, as if a sword is being driven through her chest.

'You failed to shut the little monkey up. Now I will shut it up.'

'No, no. No, I beg you, let me have her back and I will calm her.'

'You want this thing?' Otti lifts the baby higher and her tiny limbs pump the air with each scream. 'Okay, you can have it.' He jerks his head and two soldiers step back from the woman as he tosses the baby through the air at her like a sack of beans.

I cannot find my breath.

Somehow the woman manages to catch her child, pulling her back close to her breast. She scrabbles on the ground for the blanket and the general steps forward and pins the ragged cloth to the earth with his boot, nearly crushing her fingers. She jerks her hand away just in time and stares up into his face.

He towers over her. 'I don't want to see or hear either of you again.' His voice is a lion's growl. 'Do you understand me?'

Limply she nods and I expect the rifles to be raised, or Otti to draw his revolver, but suddenly the woman is on her feet and running, her baby clutched to her chest, the blanket left under the general's boot. She runs without looking back, across the field into the jungle beyond. Miraculously, no one shoots.

I am frozen, stuck staring at the beam of sunlight catching the steel handle of the revolver on Otti's belt and making it glow like a cluster of stars. He sees me looking and is in front of me in a flash. The glare he gives me makes me feel as if I'm standing naked in the middle of a lake of ice.

'Like what you see, do you?' he snarls.

Before I can even think how to respond he punches me in the ribs. I grunt and stagger back.

'Leave him alone!' someone shouts. It's Philip's voice.

Otti turns slowly. '*What?*' he demands. 'What did I just hear? Who spoke?'

No one replies. The wind holds its breath. The general takes his revolver out of its holster and fires a shot in the air.

'Who was it who spoke? Own up or you will all be shot. Right now!'

I try not to look into the dark barrels of the soldiers' rifles. I don't want to see it coming if they decide to shoot us. I glance up and see a bird with a colourful tail soaring across the sky. The clouds are so close I think I can reach out and squeeze one if I stand on tiptoe.

'It was me.'

I look back down and see Philip step forward. He stares Otti straight in the eye. 'That boy didn't do anything to you —'

The general calmly raises his gun and shoots. Philip's head snaps and his legs flip up as he falls backwards. He lies in the dirt with the dust floating over him, unmoving except for his mouth, which opens and closes like a fish out of water.

'No!' shrieks Patricia and starts towards him. She is blocked by the rebels, who forbid any of us to move. They make us stand there and watch Philip die.

Time stops altogether. I don't want him to suffer. But I don't want him to die! I watch him through blurry eyes, even though I can hardly bear to. It's all my fault, he was trying to protect me, and it would be cowardly to look away now. I can only hope that he knows how much he means to me, to all us boys, how much he's helped us. Oh God, where are you now?

When Philip is dead Otti turns back to me.

Do I care if he shoots me too? I already feel half dead inside. But I can't leave Mama, Nyanbuot, Thiko . . . Please don't shoot, I say in my head. My neck is tense and my throat is dry. At last the general motions his men to stand down.

I am spared. I don't know why, any more than I know why Philip was shot. But I do know now why they're called the Lord's Resistance Army. At this moment, General Otti is God. He decides who lives, who dies. I want to know what he's thinking, and at the same time I don't want to know. Is it really that easy to take a human life?

He strides away, flanked by his soldiers. They take with them all that they've looted. They go without announcement and we are left standing in lines in confusion.

I look back over at Philip. I have the crazy thought that he'll get up now that the soldiers are gone. But he just lies there in a pool of blood, dark and still.

7

We bury him, and the other dead, helping the workers from Philip's organisation. His family have told them that even if they were to take his body back home, his spirit would remain in Africa, so it's better that his body rest here. They say that this is what he would have wanted, although of course he never expected to die here.

At his graveside all the boys from the football teams gather, and each face asks a thousand questions that have no answer. Philip's body, wrapped in a white cloth, is lowered into the gaping hole. Stones fall, then clods and then the soil, until the grave is filled and firmed up into a sad mound, and the earth doesn't care.

It doesn't say, I don't want more. It doesn't say, I've already taken enough. It just keeps swallowing. It has swallowed Philip. It has taken him out of existence like an ant lying by the roadside. The fact that he was here to help us makes his death different somehow. Are any of us safe now?

Fog looms over everything, shrouding it in a thick grey. It covers the sun and suffocates every blade of grass and tree. It absorbs the sounds of birdsong that should be filling the air.

We walk back to our tents. I live another day. I sleep with a stomach that is empty. There are small sounds of rustling and the moan of the wind outside. As I lie on the mat between the other boys, I think about playing football with Philip. I think about Deng. I wonder if the Sudan People's Liberation Army will also come to the camp, and if Deng will be among them. I think about the last time I saw my older brother, the rage burning in his eyes the night our father was killed.

When dawn breaks, a bird sings a thin song, as if unsure it's the right time. It's answered by another, and then another, until the air is filled with the sound of them. Their chirping is calming. There's peace in their voices. It's a new day. A new day without Philip.

More UN peacekeepers arrive in the camp, but they still won't be enough to protect us if General Otti and his soldiers return.

In honour of Philip we still play football. That too is what he would have wanted, we decide. We practise, we play informal games, but I don't know if we'll ever play another big match. It just wouldn't feel right.

Our lives seem to just limp along, although I know that every day here is actually a wonderful gift and we count them, not counting down but up. There are many who haven't made it this far.

One evening, I go in search of someone I've heard about who was apparently with the Sudan People's Liberation Army but left after becoming disillusioned. I'm hoping for news of Deng, but when I find the man, nothing comes of it.

I'm on my way back, not far from our block of tents, when I see Thiko walking with a jerry can of water. Two older boys are following behind her.

'You're beautiful!' I hear one of them call to her.

'Thank you,' she replies without looking at him. She keeps walking.

'Hey!' the boy says. 'Stop. We want to know your name.'

She ignores him but the boys catch up to her. Then one grabs her arm and pulls her around. 'Come on,' he says, 'talk to us.'

'Let go of me!' Thiko slaps him away with one hand, still holding the jerry can with the other, and by the time he tries to grab her again, I've already put myself between them, shielding Thiko with my body.

'Leave her alone,' I say.

The boy looks me up and down and snickers. 'Get out of our way.'

'No,' I say, and he leans down to me.

'What did you say?' He has small, cruel eyes.

'I said back off!'

He shoves me and I punch him in the stomach. His friend grabs my wrist and though I struggle he has me pinned, and the other one grabs Thiko again. She pushes him off.

I pull loose and punch small-eyes right on the nose. He stumbles back but I feel a fist connecting with my ribs. I whirl around and punch the other boy, so hard it hurts my hand.

Blood is dripping down his face. 'He broke my nose,' he wails, and by now adults have rushed over, shouting at us to stop. Like cowards, the two boys run off.

'Are you okay?' Thiko grasps my hands, making me wince.

'Yes,' I say, though my knuckles are throbbing.

'I can't believe you punched them. They were a lot bigger than you.' I hear the awe in her voice.

'They were idiots,' I say, trying to ignore the way my hand is breathing fire through my fingernails.

'You got that one right on the nose,' Thiko giggles, and the sound of her laughing makes any pain worth it.

In the morning my hand is still throbbing. My knuckles are bruised and puffy and three of my fingers are swollen and stiff. They look like tamarind tree fruit and it's hard to close them. There's nothing for it but to try the clinic, though I'm not hopeful. They will probably say they don't have supplies and turn me away, but I go anyway.

This time I'm lucky because the line is short. I stand in the doorway, unsure who to speak to. There's no one at the desk this morning. There's a nurse checking a child's throat, and another nurse explaining to a woman how she should take the tablets she's giving her, demonstrating sunrise, midday and sunset with her hands. She looks over at me and I recognise her. She's the one who was going to treat my arm after the truck accident.

When she's finished with the woman she comes over and looks

me up and down. She sees my hand and makes a clucking noise with her tongue.

'How did this happen? Have you been in a fight?'

I look down at my feet. I don't want to tell her that I punched a boy in the face. 'Can you help me?' I ask, looking back up at her.

A smile comes to her face. 'Ah, a tough guy. I remember you now – you're the one who ran away the day you cut your arm. The day you helped Patricia. What's your name? I'm Joanna.'

I feel ashamed. She's being so kind. 'I'm Juba,' I say.

'Well, Juba, you're very brave. You possibly even saved a life. Come and sit down over here.'

'But I think you must save many lives in this clinic,' I say, following her.

'Is one life worth more than another? You save many lives by saving one.'

I think about this, and decide maybe she's right. One life isn't worth more than any other, and one person's actions can affect many.

Joanna goes away and I look around. I work out there must be about thirty beds in the two rooms, divided by partitions. When she returns she's carrying a metal basin of water, a bar of soap and a washcloth.

'Juba,' she says, 'the first thing to do is go into that little room over there and wash yourself. I know your hand hurts, but we'll be able to treat it better once all of you is cleaned up, okay?'

I look at the basin. I can't remember the last time I washed.

'Go on,' she urges. 'Wash yourself well now. I know there's nowhere for that in the camp but we can do something about it for today.'

There's such kindness in her eyes and face that I nod meekly and thank her, then go into the little room she pointed to and pull the door shut behind me. I strip off my filthy clothes and let them fall in a heap on the floor, and for a moment I just stand there, goosebumps forming on my arms even though it's not cold. I take the washcloth and dip it in the basin with the bar of soap. The water is warm and luxurious. The soap has a clean, sharp smell. I lather the suds up and wash my face, my ears, my neck, my entire body. The air tickles my skin. When I'm done, the water in the basin is brown as mud.

But I feel incredible. When was the last time I was this clean? It feels so good that I forget the pain in my hand. I realise I'm grinning as I pull on the clinic gown Joanna has left in the room. It reminds me of wearing Thiko's skirt. How long ago that seems now.

When I come out, Joanna smiles and says, 'You look much better already.' She points to the stool. 'Have a seat. You're lucky we're not so busy today.'

I sit and she examines my hand, gently squeezing and pressing. I try not to wince but it hurts.

'Are your parents here in the camp?' she asks.

'Only my mother. My father is dead, and my grandfather and my little brother. I don't know where my older brother is.'

Joanna stops pressing on my hand and holds it. 'I'm sorry,' she says. After a moment she says, 'But you live in the tent with your mother?'

'Yes, and my sister.'

'And do you have friends here?' When I nod she says, 'What are their names?'

I look at her. I can't imagine why she would want to know my friends' names.

'Why do you need to know?' I ask, and straightaway I feel bad. She's been so kind, after all, but I'm not used to someone asking me these things.

'I'm sorry,' she says, 'I know I ask a lot of questions. It's a bad habit of mine. You don't have to answer me.'

She takes a small bottle of something orange-coloured and rubs it on my hand, then bandages it. 'I can't feel anything broken but you've bruised it pretty badly and you might have a sprain. You'll have to take it easy for a few days. Try not to use your hand too much. You need to give it time to heal.'

I nod. 'Okay. Thank you.' I get up and put my clothes back on. As I walk to the door I see something familiar on the front desk. *Winnie-the-Pooh*. Another well-worn copy, just like the one Miss Ayen gave me in that other lifetime. My heart hurts along with my hand as I stare at it.

Joanna sees me looking. 'Do you know that book?' she asks. 'It's one of my favourites. I didn't bring too many personal things with me but I wanted to bring that. Sometimes I read a chapter before I go to sleep at night.'

'I've read it,' I say. 'I used to have a copy. My teacher gave it to me. It was one of her favourites too.' I think of the last time I saw Miss Ayen and I close my eyes, trying to rid my mind of the image.

'You must miss going to school,' Joanna says.

'I do. I liked it a lot. I like learning new things.'

She considers me for a moment. 'Juba, how would you like a job? Do you think you could help me out around here? Keep the place clean, roll bandages?' She tells me that the clinic has two rooms for the medical and nursing staff, a storeroom, and even a room for intensive care. Along with the rooms for the patients.

Can this be true? Or is it a trap? She seems sincere.

'I can't pay you,' she continues, 'but I can offer quick treatment if you or any of your family get sick.' She leans towards me. 'And I can get you a ration card too, if you don't have one. Do you?'

My head is spinning. It's too good to be true. Joanna must be stringing me along.

'Are you just saying that?' I ask at last.

She raises an eyebrow. 'I never lie during working hours.'

I'm so happy right now I can't think of anything to say.

'I'll take that smile as a yes. Now, there are a few things you should know first.' The way Joanna says this reminds me again of Miss Ayen. 'I'm the head nurse and there are four other nurses who work with me. I expect you to follow any instructions they give you, but it's my word that's final.'

She walks over to the medicine cupboard and pulls out one of the little orange bottles. 'This is Mercurochrome,' she says. 'We use it to help prevent infection. So now if I ask you to fetch it for me, you'll know what it looks like. We use other things too of course, and I'll teach you about those as time goes on, but this is one of the most important.'

I am overcome with the desire to do well here, to make Joanna glad she's trusted me.

'But for now,' she goes on, 'go back to your tent and rest that hand. You can come back in three days and I'll see if it's healed enough for you to start work.'

I can barely get through those days but I do my best to avoid using my right hand. After three days I'm back at the clinic first thing, before any line has formed. Joanna checks my hand and agrees to let me begin work.

'Your first job,' she tells me, 'is to scrub your clothes clean. Put fresh water in the basin in the little room and use this.' She hands me a scrubbing brush with stiff yellow bristles. 'Put a little soap on it and scrub, but not so hard that you tear the fabric. You can hang them out the back – you'll find a line strung across branches. Once you've finished that, report back to me and I'll give you your next job.' She hands me a fresh shirt and trousers to wear in the meantime.

I set about my task and have just returned from hanging up my clothes when a woman comes into the clinic. She has a round-faced little girl with her who sags listlessly against her mother, eyes dull.

'She's burning up,' Joanna says, feeling her. 'Help me get her to the cot,' she says to the mother.

But as they do, the girl collapses. Her mother catches her and with Joanna carries her to the cot. The girl's breathing is laboured and her eyes have rolled back in her head. Joanna calls out for the other nurses and two hurry in. The girl's skinny arms and legs have gone limp. Joanna feels for a pulse, then shakes her head.

Tears well in the mother's eyes but she doesn't wail or throw herself on the ground like women usually do when their children die. The nurses step back and the mother kneels by her daughter, leans down and kisses her. She prays.

Only a minute or two has passed before two men come in, wrap the girl in a white sheet and remove the body. Even though I've seen people die before, I'm shocked that this death has happened so quickly. One moment the little girl was here and the next she was not. My throat closes like a fist. My excitement about the job vanishes, and when Joanna assigns me further tasks I do them numbly.

When it's time to go I put my clean clothes back on and ask Joanna what time she would like me there the following day.

'How about eight o'clock?'

'Sure.'

'This isn't an easy job,' she says, eyeing me. 'You'll see many things you wish you hadn't. But you did very well today, Juba. Thank you.'

I nod and go to leave.

'Wait,' she says. 'You're forgetting something. Close the door a minute, please.'

I do so, even though I don't know what she's talking about. She opens her desk, pulls something out and hands it to me. It's a ration card. My stomach jumps, as if it's already sensing the food to come.

'Guard this carefully,' she says, as my fingers close around it. 'Don't tell anyone where you got it from. Another worker gave it to you, if someone asks. You take this to the food tent tonight and get some food for your family, okay?'

'Thank you,' I whisper. 'For everything.'

My mood lifted, I run back to the tent, thinking of the look on Mama and Nyanbuot's faces when I show them the card.

I call them outside and we crouch behind the tent. Mama thinks I'm being silly until I pull the card out of my pocket. Her eyes widen in disbelief and Nyanbuot jumps up and down.

'Let's go to get the food right now,' she says, wriggling with joy.

We do, and we eat, trying to pace ourselves so we don't get sick. From now on, we will each get seventeen pounds of grain every month and nearly a pint of cooking oil, also four pounds of dried beans or lentils. This seems unbelievable after going so long without enough food.

I tell Mama about what I do at the clinic but I don't tell her about the dead girl.

'My clever young man,' Mama whispers, touching my arm. 'Look at you. I am so proud of you.' The only other time I've seen such light in Mama's eyes is when she talks about my father. She would speak about him all day if someone was there to listen.

That night, lying on my mat with a full stomach for the first time in many months, I can't stop thinking of my father. The war had been going on for a long time when he was murdered, but to me, to my family, that was the first day of the war.

And when Thon-Gool was killed, the war crept even closer. How well I remember that day too.

I had been working in the garden, with my dog nearby, when Grandpa called me to come and help prepare a fish for supper. I ran to make sure the fire was ready while Grandpa cut down a fish. Whenever Grandpa caught a fish, he would dry it in the sun and then hang it up to cure. He liked to cure his fish for a long time, which meant they developed a pungent scent and started to rot. Eventually the flies stopped landing on them and the maggots stopped curling through their flesh. The fish made a great soup after this.

That day, Thon-Gool, after a wagging, prancing greeting, flopped down by Grandpa's four-legged stool.

'Grandpa, did you know I can run faster than Chieng or Majok or any other boy in the village?' I said as I prodded the coals.

Grandpa was refining the edge of his spear at the grindstone. He turned his head to give me his sideways smile, half amused, half stern. 'The boasting man shows conceit over wisdom, Juba.'

Thon-Gool raised his ears and cocked his head as if listening to us.

'But it's not a boast, Grandpa,' I said. 'It's the truth.'

Grandpa chuckled. 'A man who neither lies nor boasts has the wisdom to take pride in his achievements without pointing them out to those around him.'

When I heard movement outside a few minutes later I thought it must be Mama, Thon and Nyanbuot back from fetching water. I was still mulling over what Grandpa had said as I stepped to the door to greet them, but it flew open before I reached it and a man with a gun came in. He was followed by two others.

I had never seen men like these up close before. They scanned the hut with eyes like wild animals. Grandpa told me later they were Sudan People's Liberation Army rebels.

Grandpa's grindstone screeched to a halt. Thon-Gool barked and leapt forward, baring his teeth, and Grandpa restrained him, putting his arm around him and scratching his back. The dog stayed quiet for a moment, until the rebels started throwing things around, searching through the groceries. Thon-Gool growled and one of the men lifted his rifle to Thon-Gool's face and fired.

A deafening noise filled the hut and a strangled yelp escaped from Thon-Gool. Something hot and sloppy sprayed over my face and arms.

Then it was my own scream hammering in my ears. I went to throw myself at the rebel, yelling like a tortured child, but Grandpa, his speed belying his years, leapt between us and knocked me down, sending me sprawling onto my backside.

In front of me, my dog's blood streamed onto the floor from his nose and head. His beautiful brown eyes were dimming. His feet clawed the air in a last movement as his life drained away.

How could Thon-Gool die? He was my best friend.

The rebel's eyes lit up. He grinned, showing ragged yellow teeth. The other two shouted and pounded on the walls of the hut with the butts of their guns. Hyenas would not yap like that over a kill. A red haze of anger floated before my eyes.

The man who'd killed Thon-Gool shook his rifle at me. 'Get up!' he ordered. 'Get up now, boy!'

I rose onto my elbows and he pushed Grandpa aside to shove me in the chest with the stock of his gun. I fell back breathless with pain.

'Come on then, get up!'

'Leave him alone,' Grandpa said, fear making the tendons in his neck stand out. 'He's only a boy.'

'Shut up, old man,' the rebel ordered. He grabbed my arm and yanked me to my feet as if I weighed nothing. 'Stand up straight!' He cuffed me across the ear and I saw stars. 'I said stand up!'

I managed to struggle to my feet and a cold ripple of horror passed through me as the rebel squatted down.

'You think you're brave, do you?' He ran his thumb along my spine, like a doctor searching for a disease, commanding me to stand taller, then he pulled my face around by my chin. The stink of him and the blood of my dog mixed in a nauseating odour. I fought the need to be sick.

'Lucky you're short,' he snarled. 'But you'll be taller and stronger soon, boy. And when you are you'll join us. We'll destroy the corrupt Sudanese government together and free our country.'

I swallowed, trying to control my fear. 'I . . . I don't want to be a soldier,' I said, the words sticking in my throat.

This was met with loud laughter by all three. The man in front of me gripped my arm and shook me like a dog shakes a squirrel. 'You'll change your mind when the Arabs come,' he said. 'When the Arabs pillage a pretty village like yours, what they leave behind will stay in your memory for the rest of your life. That is, if you live at all.' He let go of me with a jerk.

Lying here in the tent, I think how that rebel was right. What the government soldiers did to Pacong will never leave me. But at least tonight I can fall sleep without hunger pains. Not even the snores of the other boys on my mat dampen that.

8

Every morning now I go to work at the clinic, and every day I learn something new. I had forgotten what it feels like to learn things, to use my mind for something other than worrying about where to find the next meal. And I'd forgotten how good it is to share food with people. We can do that now we have a ration card.

Soon I can roll bandages like a professional. There are so many people coming into the clinic, all day, every day. They have malaria, pneumonia or diarrhoea, they've been bitten by a snake or they've broken bones or sprained their ankle. They're all malnourished.

But not everyone who comes in is actually sick. Two of our patients this morning were girls. One was carrying a young baby. They smiled shyly at Joanna as they told her they needed a certain type of help. I heard the words 'birth control'. I knew that most South Sudanese women and girls don't talk about this kind of thing in open places, and Joanna must have known this too because she took them into a back room. I wasn't sure whether I was allowed to follow but I did anyway, and no one protested.

Joanna showed the girls the different products and explained how they work. The girls giggled and covered their faces when Joanna demonstrated a condom on her finger. They left happy, still giggling.

I've quickly learnt the routine here at the clinic. I start at 7.30, when the people who were on night shift go home to sleep. We treat the emergencies first, if there are any, then give priority to children.

After a month or so, Joanna tells me I'm a natural at this work, which makes me smile proudly. But I don't smile when she calls me Nurse Juba.

'I'm not a girl,' I say. 'Boys can't be nurses.'

'Is that so?' She raises an eyebrow. 'Who told you that?'

No one has told me that, but the only nurses I've ever known of have been women. 'Are there nurses that are men?' I ask.

'There are.'

Really? I wonder, in that case, if I *could* be a nurse too.

A little later a man comes in with a wounded shoulder that needs stitching. It's one of the many things Joanna does in the clinic that fascinate me. She can stitch someone's skin as easily as Mama darns clothing. I want to be able to do that, I think as I watch her. When she's finished, she puts ointment and a bandage over the stitches and the man gives her a toothless grin.

'Do you think I could learn to stitch people like that?' I ask when he's left.

'Absolutely you could,' she says. 'You're a quick learner, Juba, and you have a good manner with the patients. I think maybe you could go to nursing school one day, when this is all over.'

Nursing school! I can't believe she just said that.

'Do you really mean it?'

She nods eagerly. 'Like I said, you've got a natural aptitude for this work.'

'I could be a nurse who also tells stories,' I say.

'Sometimes that's the best medicine! Getting people to smile, helping them forget their problems. I think you'd be a very good nurse.'

It's nearly the end of my shift, so I gather up stray bandages and put medicine bottles away. Having this job, being of some help to people, makes the camp almost bearable. Joanna is such a good, kind person, with a warmth that lights her eyes. When she smiles I can't help smiling too.

When I've finished cleaning up I say goodbye and hurry back to our tent, eager to tell Mama and Nyanbuot that I'm going to learn how to do stitches. They're both so happy for me that I decide to go and tell Thiko too. Because of the clinic I haven't seen as much of her lately.

She's not in her tent. I can't find Chieng either, so I go in search of Majok. When I mention Thiko a curious look comes over his face.

'So have you seen her?' I ask.

Majok hesitates. 'I've seen her with Chieng a lot these days.'

Something about the way he says this gives me a funny feeling. 'So what?' I say. 'Thiko is allowed to hang out with who she wants.'

'Do you get days off from your job?' Majok asks. 'Let's all hang out next time you don't have to work, okay? We haven't played football in ages.'

I agree, even though I'm not sure when that might be. I head back to my tent, hoping that working at the clinic doesn't mean I will lose Thiko.

I sleep badly and wake early. To shut off bad thoughts, I get up and head straight to the clinic. Joanna is already at her desk, sipping coffee.

'Good morning,' she says. 'You're here early. You worked so hard yesterday I figured you'd still be asleep.'

I mumble something about there being too much noise in the tent and Joanna says, 'Do you like coffee?'

'I've never had coffee. It smells good, though. I've smelt it before.'

'Would you like to try some?'

Of course I would, and she goes over to the little kitchen area and pours me a cup.

'I haven't put any milk in it,' she says as she sets it in front of me. 'If you get used to drinking it black from the start, you'll never know what you're missing. I prefer my coffee black anyway.'

I take a tentative sip. It's hot and bitter tasting, but at the same time delicious too. Once I've drunk it all, I can see why it's the thing you'd want to start your morning with.

Joanna has been watching me. She gets up again and comes back with a yellow cardboard box, a bowl and a spoon, and sets them on her desk. I can tell it's food by the picture on the box but I wonder what kind of food comes in a big yellow box.

She tips the box over the bowl and tiny brown objects in the shape of the letter O spill out. 'Cheerios,' she says. 'Cereal. You do have to add milk to this, though.' She returns to the kitchen area and puts two spoonfuls of powder into a mug, adds some water to it and stirs.

When she brings the mug out I stare at it. It's watery and a little lumpy.

'That doesn't look like any milk I've had before,' I say.

'It's not as good as fresh milk, it's true. But it will make your cereal taste better.' She pours the milk into my bowl. 'Enjoy.'

The first couple of bites I take are crunchy, but the Cheerios soften in the milk. Even though it's not milk from our goats, it's the best breakfast I've had in a long time. And it came out of that yellow cardboard box!

At the end of the day I go in search of Chieng and find him sitting outside his tent, drawing in the dirt with a stick. I remember how he used to do that all the time.

We talk a little awkwardly for a while and then he says, 'I've been thinking. I don't want to stay here anymore. Who does, right? I'm going back.'

I'm not sure what he means. 'Going back where?'

'To Pacong,' he says.

I stare at him. 'Pacong is gone, Chieng. There's nowhere to go, that's why we're here. We're refugees.'

He spits in the dirt. 'I hate that word. *Refugee*.'

'So? I don't like it either. No one does. But that's the truth you have to live with. You don't have a home right now, except here.'

'This will never be my home! It's not yours either. Although maybe it is, since you have a job and everything.' His eyes narrow. 'Anyway, I'm going back. I'll find a group of Sudan People's Liberation Army soldiers and join them.'

I can't believe what I'm hearing. 'You don't mean that. You're going to become a rebel?'

'You don't think I can?'

I try to stay calm. 'Chieng, I think you can do anything if you put your mind to it,' I say slowly. 'But why would you want to join those people? They're murderers.'

'What else am I supposed to do? Sit here and starve? We're wasting away. They've got us all rounded up in here and no one is doing anything. I want to do something. Somebody has to.'

I can't imagine Chieng as a rebel. 'But *you* don't have to,' I say.

He gives me a level look. 'Who will then?'

'I don't know. Someone else.'

'And that's the problem. Everyone wants to leave it up to someone else and so nothing gets done. I heard the LRA rebels will come back. The Ugandans know there are young people here who can fight. I don't want to get kidnapped and be forced to join them. I'd rather join the good guys, the South Sudan rebels, to fight for my country. For our freedom.'

'But those guys are no good either,' I say. 'They're just as much killers.'

Then Chieng says something that really knocks me. 'Majok is going too. I'd ask you if you wanted to as well, but I think I already know your answer.'

His face is earnest. He looks like he means what he's saying. I feel like I don't know who he is anymore.

'If you want to come with us, you can,' he says. 'It's the right thing to do.'

'You're crazy.'

'Oh, so you think it's fine that the Sudanese government is murdering our people? You think it's okay that they're bombing schools and burning villages? And we should all just stay out of their way and let them do what they want? We should run, not stand up and fight? Is that how you want to live?'

'I don't think that,' I tell him. 'You know I don't. Of course I don't think what they did is okay! And yes, they need to be stopped. But by armies. By adults.' I pause. 'We're kids, Chieng. We should be playing football, not going to war.'

For a moment it seems my words have resonated, but then he shakes his head.

'Majok and I are going to do it. There are two others coming with us. You think we should leave this to the adults, but what have they done so far? Built this camp where they're keeping all of us, that's what they've done. We're going to do something real.'

I can't meet his eyes. But I force myself to, and when I do I see there will be no talking him out of this. His mind is made up.

'Our country needs us, Juba,' he says. 'Come with us. Make a difference. We'll join the Sudan People's Liberation Army and be rebels together.'

'My mother and sister need me too. And you're going to get killed if you do this, Chieng.'

'Do what?' says Thiko.

Where has she come from?

'Chieng is going off to join the rebels!' I tell her.

He stands up and moves towards me. He has a dark look on his face. 'Come with us, Juba. You know it's the right thing to do. I'm challenging you to do what's right!'

Thiko steps between us. 'Are you out of your mind?' she asks Chieng. 'Do you want to become a killer and a rapist? Do you want to loot and burn? Didn't we talk about this the other day? You'll never go back to school. You'll never be anything more than one of them until you're dead. Which won't take long, because what do you know about fighting?' Her voice is calm but her eyes are blazing.

'Don't act like you know everything, Miss Smarty,' Chieng says with a sneer. 'Are we in school now?'

'No, but nor are we smoking and drinking blood and swearing oaths to have no mercy on any soul, like those insane rebels. We're staying alive and keeping together until we can rebuild a village. That's something worth fighting for! If you want to die, go ahead and join the rebels, but leave Juba out of it.' Her hand closes around mine.

Chieng laughs bitterly. 'You two should get married and set up house in this camp for the rest of your lives. I'm sure you'd be very happy.'

He looks pointedly at Thiko and says, 'You stay out of this, little girl.' Then he turns back to me. 'When the Ugandans come next time, they'll take you away. Better to join our rebels voluntarily. Unless you're afraid. Are you afraid?'

This boy standing in front of me now is not the boy I've known my whole life. Part of me wants to jump on him and pummel him. But a part of me also wonders if he's right. Maybe it *is* better to march into the lion's den than to be dragged there like a man already dead?

But those rebels kill people. They killed my dog. I don't want to become one of them.

'Well?' Chieng says impatiently. '*Are* you afraid?'

He has lost his family. He has seen horrible things that will never leave his memory. He doesn't know what he's saying.

'I won't be the person who takes away someone's father or brother,' I tell him, and he spits again.

'You're a coward. A little girl all along, like the rebel said.'

This is not your friend, I tell myself. This is not the real Chieng talking, this is a boy who's become twisted by having lost too much.

'You can only die once and it's better to die doing what's right,' he says.

Where has he been hearing this stuff?

'I don't see how killing more innocent people is going to make anything right. And what you're saying isn't right either, Chieng. I don't know what the answer is but it's not that.'

He looks at me with scorn. 'Those are the words of a boy who once wore a skirt. Who should *still* be wearing a skirt. Waahh!' Chieng howls like a baby, rubbing his fists into his eyes. 'Your little sister would make a better man than you.'

He walks away, then turns around. 'As for your grandpa,' he calls, 'he died for nothing.'

I reach him in a flash. 'Take that back!' I shout.

Thiko rushes after me and tries to intervene but it's too late, I'm on top of Chieng, hitting and punching. He lashes out at me but I feel nothing. I clutch his head, imprisoning it under my arm, but he pulls himself free and manages to get on top of me. He grabs my neck and squeezes it, making it hard to breathe.

Other boys have gathered to watch now, and Thiko is screaming at us to stop. I throw punches at Chieng's chest and face, making contact with his temple. He jerks his head into my chin and I let out a low cry as the pain spreads across my jaw and up my face. I feel dizzy and I'm sweating.

At last he lets go and rolls off me. We're both panting like dogs. I get up and gasp, 'My grandfather saved my life. I'd be dead many times over if it hadn't been for him. My mother and sister would have no one. Don't ever dare say he died for nothing again!'

Blood trickles from Chieng's nose, and one eye is already swelling. 'I know,' he says. 'I'm sorry. I shouldn't have said that.'

'There's a lot more you shouldn't have said, Chieng.' Thiko's voice is cold.

He glances at her as he brushes himself off and then looks at me. 'You're stronger than I thought.' He holds his hand out to shake, which I do, cautiously.

'Chieng,' I say, 'I know how hard it is here, especially for you. You don't know where your mother is . . . But what's the point of causing more hurt and pain?'

He looks miserable. 'You're right,' he says. 'I know you're right. It's just so frustrating being trapped here doing nothing, being powerless.'

I search his face. 'Does my being right mean you'll stay?' I ask.

He nods. 'I'll stay.' Then, after a moment, 'For now at least.'

As Thiko and I leave she says, 'I'm so glad you talked him out of it. Could you imagine him and Majok with the rebels?'

'Majok told me you and Chieng have been hanging out,' I blurt. I had planned to give this more thought, to decide exactly what to say when I brought it up, but the words are out of my mouth before I know it. My face burns.

Thiko stares at me. 'Majok said that?' She sounds like she's about to laugh. 'Boys like to gossip as much as women do!'

'So you're . . . you're not hanging out?'

'No. We've spent time together because I've been trying to talk him out of his stupid ideas. He seems to believe he can single-handedly bring peace to Sudan. But Juba, I wish it could've been the two of us talking to him. I think he would have seen reason a lot sooner if you'd been around.'

That makes me feel a bit guilty. 'Well, I've been busy at the clinic.'

'I know. And I'm glad you have a job there but I do miss getting to see you.'

She slips her warm hand in mine and I'm so relieved she isn't lost to me.

9

Next morning the clinic is full when I get there, mostly with children. The lack of clean water in the camp is causing sickness. Joanna is giving a boy malaria tablets when the door opens and a woman runs in screaming.

'Come! Come with me!' she cries, grabbing Joanna by the arm. 'Hurry, please, my daughter is dying.'

The doctors have their hands full, so Joanna grabs her bag and rushes out. I stop what I'm doing and race after her.

A crowd has gathered around a tent. People step aside to let Joanna and the woman pass and I follow behind them. Inside, a child, perhaps a year old, is lying motionless on the ground.

'Help her!' begs the man beside her, and Joanna kneels down and makes a quick assessment. Then she tilts the little head back and pinches the nose and puts her mouth over the girl's mouth, pushing air into the tiny body. She places both hands on the girl's sternum, one on top of the other, and pumps her chest. This seems to go on for a lifetime. I can hear people outside the tent praying. I'm wondering how long Joanna will continue to do this when suddenly the girl's arm twitches. Her eyes flutter and she coughs and sputters. She starts to cry and her mother is right there, reaching for her, tears rolling down.

Joanna rocks back on her heels and wipes her forehead. I can only stare in awe. At last she picks up the baby and stands.

'Juba, you bring my bag. I need to take her to the clinic to see a doctor.'

'What's wrong with her?' I ask as we walk back.

'I'm not entirely sure,' she says. 'That's why I want a doctor to have a look at her.'

'Well, that was just amazing,' I tell her, but she only smiles and brushes off the praise.

I'm still in awe when we return to the clinic, where our day does not slow down. Just after lunch, a pregnant woman bursts in, a pained expression on her sweating face.

'I'm in labour early,' she gasps. 'I didn't think the baby would be here for another few weeks. I was hoping we wouldn't be in the camp by then but it looks like this baby has other plans.'

Joanna jumps up. 'Come on, Juba. Here's your first lesson in obstetrics.'

I'm not sure what that is but I follow Joanna as she helps the woman onto a cot.

The woman doesn't want to lie down for long. 'Here comes another one,' she says, gritting her teeth. She pushes herself off the cot and paces back and forth, pulling at her threadbare dress. She finally pulls it off completely. Her body is both startling and beautiful, her belly huge and round and tight as a drum.

'Her contractions are getting closer and closer together,' Joanna tells me. 'The baby will be here soon.'

When there's a break between contractions, Joanna has the woman lie back on the cot. She puts on a glove and slides her hand into the woman. It looks painful but the woman doesn't appear to even notice. Her eyes are closed.

'Oh yes,' Joanna says, sliding her hand back out. 'Get ready to push, Mama, because this baby is on the way.'

She turns to me. 'Juba, will you go and get some extra blankets and towels, please.'

I fetch what she wants and rush back to find the woman on her hands and knees on the cot, rocking back and forth. She's moaning, and it sounds a little like singing, but then the moan ends in an anguished cry. She's quiet for a moment, until it all starts over.

Joanna talks to her softly, though I can tell by the look on the woman's face she's not listening. It's like she's in trance, aware only of the feelings in her body.

I think about this baby who is about to be born here, in a refugee camp. This is not what the mother would have envisioned when she fell pregnant. Yet it is happening.

'You're doing great,' Joanna says. 'Wait for a contraction before you push again, okay? And remember to breathe. Look, Juba, the baby's about to crown.'

I stand there watching, feeling helpless and awestruck. The top of the baby's head appears and then disappears several times before it finally slips out far enough that it doesn't go back at the end of the contraction. The skin at the top of the skull is puckered, smeared with blood and something white. The woman howls. She sounds like an animal. She pushes twice more and then the head is all the way out. Another two pushes and the body slips out easily in a rush of fluid. The umbilical cord is like a thick, pulsing serpent.

The woman gives a shout of relief. The baby is quiet for a second, its mouth open, eyes squeezed shut. Then it wails.

'It's a girl!' Joanna says. The woman turns over and Joanna places the baby on her chest. She drapes a blanket over the baby, and the mother can't stop smiling down at her new daughter, who is wrinkly and funny-looking, but it's unmistakable how much love the woman has for her.

Joanna can't stop smiling either, and I think I even catch her wiping a tear from her eye. It is truly wonderful, I think, the way life goes on. No matter where you are.

Joanna looks at me. She must have read my thoughts because she says, 'I've helped a lot of labouring women and it never fails to amaze me how miraculous life is.'

The day has made me think of what Nathan Waterman used to say about how important education is. I might not be going to school anymore but I'm still learning, and I'm getting a lot of hands-on experience, which is maybe even better than school. I think Nathan would be happy for me.

One day follows the next at the clinic. I can change bandages by myself now, which gives me great confidence. When a young girl comes in after a fall with a long laceration on her upper arm and a sprained ankle, Joanna explains to me exactly what she's doing as she stitches her arm and then has me feel the ligament in the ankle. She gets me to gently run my fingers over it to see whether it's torn.

'I don't think it is,' I say. 'It feels swollen and tender to me, but not torn.'

'You're right,' says Joanna. 'It's stretched but it hasn't torn.' She smiles at the girl. 'So that's good. We're going to keep you here with your ankle elevated and iced for now, and then Juba will show you how to bandage it properly for support. It should start to feel better in a few days.'

I wrap ice packs around the ankle and then bandage it, explaining as I go. When I'm done the girl looks at me and says, 'Thank you, Doctor.'

It's hard not to smile at that, both at the idea and from the pride I feel. 'I'm not a doctor,' I tell her.

'He's not a doctor yet,' Joanna says. 'But I bet he will be one day.'

So I've gone from potential nurse to potential doctor? My head spins.

At the end of the day, when the girl's brother has accompanied her back to their tent, Joanna asks me to restock the supply shelves. I organise the latex gloves, the antiseptic swabs, the gauze. I'm carrying a box of Mercurochrome when I slip. I don't know if there was a wet spot on the floor or what, but my legs go right out from under me and the box flies out of my hands. I make a grab for it but it crashes to the ground. The bottles of Mercurochrome shatter.

Joanna comes running. 'What was —?' Her voice cuts off when she sees the broken bottles all over the floor. 'Oh *no*.'

She drops to her hands and knees, even though there's no way she'll be able to salvage any of it. 'Juba, that was our entire supply!'

I'm speechless with horror at what I've done. 'I'm . . . I'm sorry, Joanna,' I manage to say. 'It was an accident. I'm sorry.'

She rocks back on her heels. 'I know,' she says. I can hear how upset she is. 'But Juba, you need to be more careful with things like this. It'll be weeks before I'm able to get any more. This is not good. Not good.' She looks around and sighs. 'Please get a broom and dustpan and start cleaning this up. I don't want anyone getting hurt on the broken glass.'

My hip smarts from where I landed on it but I figure I deserve this pain. I blink back hot tears of shame. I've let Joanna down and I hate it. I hate having her upset with me. I *should* have been more careful. Or I should at least have caught the box. Saved at least one or two of the bottles. But every one of them is smashed, and that medicine is so important.

All I can think of as I sweep up the glass is what a waste it is. Maybe I won't make such a good doctor.

Joanna says everyone has accidents and I shouldn't be too hard on myself. This makes me feel a little better, but three days later the girl with the sprained ankle is back because the stitches in her arm have become infected. The skin around them is swollen and oozing pus. She has a fever.

Joanna looks grim. 'We'll just have to do the best we can with what we've got,' she says.

What we've got are antiseptic wipes and no Mercurochrome. By noon the girl's temperature is close to 104 degrees. We've given her paracetamol and plenty of water but this hasn't reduced her fever. I put cool cloths on her forehead. I gently swab at her arm again, even though the infection has moved well beyond the surface where the wipes can reach. Joanna says there's nothing more we can do and goes to tend others waiting for treatment. Even the clinic doctors say they can do nothing further.

The girl is delirious. 'Mama?' she says. She told us the first day we treated her that her mother had been killed. Is her mother's spirit here at the clinic? Is that what she's seeing?

'I want to go home,' she whispers. 'Can I please go home now?' She looks right at me, her face flushed, and I swallow the lump in my throat and nod.

'You can go home,' I tell her.

'I don't think I know how to get there.'

'I bet you can find your way.'

'No, I can't remember.' She's beginning to writhe on the cot.

'I think the way home is down past the river,' I tell her. 'You follow the river for a little while and then there's a path you take, through the grasslands.'

The girl's eyes close. 'Grasslands,' she repeats.

'Yes. And you follow that path up a hill. When you reach the top, you'll be able to see your whole village. Nestled among the hills that lie like pillows on the land, with the grass flattened under the wind, shimmering in waves. If you look hard enough, you'll be able to see your hut.'

'I can see it,' she says. 'I can see the flowers. And the butterflies.'

'You're almost there. Follow the butterflies. They will lead you to your family and friends. They're all there, waiting for you.'

A faint smile touches the corners of her mouth. Her face relaxes into a vision of calm. 'Thank you, Doctor,' she whispers.

That's the last thing she says. I sit with her for another hour, listening to her laboured breathing, holding her hand. Then she is still. She's gone. Just like that.

I know death happens every day. That's how it is. There isn't a single family in this camp that's intact. But now I'm one of the bringers of death. How am I any better than a murderer?

I don't go back to the clinic for several days. I can't bring myself to go. My guilt is like a gigantic brick someone has placed on top of me.

'Doesn't Joanna need you at the clinic?' Mama asks.

'Not today,' I say listlessly.

She tilts my chin up and looks into my eyes. 'Juba, did something happen there?'

I swallow. I've told no one about my clumsiness, about the girl who died. The girl who died because of me.

'I killed someone,' I say at last.

Mama's eyes widen. 'Juba! What on earth do you mean?'

'I dropped all the Mercurochrome when I was putting it away and because of that a girl's wound got infected and she died.'

'Oh Juba,' Mama says. 'That death is not your fault.'

'Yes it *is*. How can you say it's not my fault? If I hadn't dropped the box of Mercurochrome, we would have been able to give her that and stopped the infection. She'd still be alive.'

'My son, you cannot go around blaming yourself like this,' Mama says sadly. 'Otherwise you'll never be able to get up and face the morning again. You must forgive yourself. And you don't know for sure that she would have lived, even if you'd given her the medicine. Maybe she would have, but maybe not. Many people die even after getting medicine. God determines these things, not you. You were trying to do good, Juba. You were trying to help people.'

Mama has been stroking my hair as she talks. Now she stops and says, 'Tell me, were you with this girl when she died?'

I nod.

'And did you sit by her, hold her hand?'

'Yes. I told her a little story.'

'What was it about?'

I can hardly bear to remember. 'About going home,' I say. 'She wanted to go home and she didn't know how.'

Mama smiles. 'Then I would say you helped this girl far more than you're giving yourself credit for. And I think if you could ask this girl, she would say she's grateful for what you did. You could only do what you were able to do. Juba, I don't want to see you lying around like this. You have important work to do. It's not always going to go perfectly, that's the way of the world. But you cannot give up. Do you understand me?'

Mama's tone has grown stern. I know she's right. And I'm so glad she's completely back to her old strong self now, after those awful first months in the camp. I want her to stay this way.

'Besides,' she says, 'you're not going to do anyone any good if you never leave this tent again.' She gives me a hug. 'I want you to know how proud I am of you. I really am. And your father and your grandfather would be too.'

Joanna is at her desk when I arrive. It's quiet for once, with only a few people lying on the cots.

'Juba,' she says, looking up and putting down her pen. 'I wasn't sure if I was going to see you today or not. Why don't you sit for a minute? Has everything been okay?'

I take a seat. 'You're probably wondering why I didn't show up for a few days.'

'I was a little worried, yes. I was thinking of coming to see you.'

'I . . . I didn't know if I could come back.'

Joanna looks sad. 'You know, Juba, I need to apologise to you, because I was too harsh. It could just as easily have been me who slipped.'

'No, you wouldn't have done that.'

She gives me a keen look. 'Don't be so sure. I don't need to tell you that this work is stressful. And sometimes the stress can get to you, and I think I let it get to me that day. It was wrong of me to make you feel bad about something you didn't do on purpose.'

'But if I hadn't done it, that girl would still be alive. You can't change that fact.'

'It wasn't the lack of Mercurochrome that caused the girl's death,' says Joanna. 'Sometimes there are deaths that we just can't explain. That's the thing about this kind of work. We can do our best and it's not enough. It's never easy to lose a patient. And there are always going to be what-ifs running through your mind, that's normal, but you can't let them overwhelm you. You're doing a great job here, Juba. We're not going to be able to save everyone. No one ever can. It can be hard to accept that.'

I sigh. 'That's sort of along the lines of what Mama told me.'

Joanna smiles. 'Well, she's right.'

'So . . . you still want me to come here every day?'

'Want you to? Of course I do, I *need* you to. You're an important part of this clinic, Juba, whether you realise it or not.'

Joanna goes on to tell me about a girl she employed in the past who was a good worker but stole medicine. She was replaced with a man who couldn't take orders from a woman.

So it's settled. I'm back on the job. I'm so relieved. I know that having this work is what's stopping me from going crazy in the camp.

And as soon as I think that, I feel sad for everyone who isn't so lucky, all the others here who have nothing to do. No wonder they end up sitting in the dirt and staring at space.

People come to the clinic after getting cut, bitten or stung. Or because they're dehydrated, or they need stitches and bandaging. Sometimes, when it's not so busy, they come in only because they want someone to give them attention, be kind to them.

Things go well and I regain my confidence. We get a new delivery of Mercurochrome. Joanna is so good to work with that I think how I want her to stay here forever, and then have to remind myself that I don't want to stay here forever. I wonder if she knows how much she's changed things for me, the hope she's given me, something I never thought I'd find here in the camp. She's come to feel like a sister. But I don't have the right words to tell her this.

At the end of one particularly busy day, she comes up to me holding out a red can with silver writing on it. I've seen cans, and bottles, like this before but I've never tasted what's inside.

'This is for you,' Joanna says. 'For working so hard. Have you had a Coke before?'

I shake my head and she shows me how to pop the tab on the can. The hiss makes me jump. I take a sip and feel my whole face light up. It's so harshly sweet in the most pleasant way, tickling my throat as I swallow. Then without warning I burp, loudly. I cover my mouth, eyes wide with embarrassment. But only for a second, because both Joanna and I burst into giggles.

'It can have that effect,' she says.

Even though I want to gulp the whole thing down, I make myself save half, tucking it under my shirt as I leave the clinic.

Joanna asks if she can walk with me to my tent. 'I'd like to meet your mother,' she says. 'Tell her what a great job you've been doing.'

As we walk she tells me about her own family. One brother and one sister. Joanna is the oldest.

I wonder why her family has only three children. If my father were alive, I'd have a lot more brothers and sisters, maybe even as many as my cousin, who has a hundred and sixty brothers and forty sisters. His father has eighty-six wives. I tell Joanna about him.

She laughs. 'Eighty-six! That's a lot of wives to take care of. And a lot of siblings to bicker with.'

'You will be a good wife,' I blurt out. 'Then a good mother after that. The kind of mother every kid wants.'

She laughs heartily at that. 'You think so? My boyfriend wouldn't agree with you. He doesn't think I'll be a good wife at all. I'll have to tell him you said that.'

'Where is your boyfriend?' I try to imagine what he might be like, this person who thinks Joanna wouldn't be a good wife.

'He's in Australia.'

Australia! We were starting to study this country just before our school got bombed. We only had one class on it, but I saw a picture of an amazing building there. I don't remember what it was but it was shaped like shells put on top of each other. Majok thought it looked like crazy slices of mango.

'He must miss you a lot,' I say.

'He does. I miss him too.'

Joanna is pretty, and I know that girls like her cost a lot in dowry. 'How many cows will he pay to your parents?' I ask.

'Cows?' She laughs. 'Oh Juba, he's not going to pay anything. Definitely not cows.'

I stare at her. 'What do you mean he won't pay anything? Not even a goat?'

'Not even a chicken.'

I've heard that this happens in other countries. From watching Oprah. But I don't understand it. How can a girl's family eat if the daughter brings no bride price?

Joanna tells me that Australian parents don't need their daughters' dowries in order to increase their wealth. The way they do marriages in Australia is opposite to how we do ours. Joanna says when a boy and a girl like each other, they meet each other's families and no one can fight the boy. The brother will do nothing. Instead of hitting his sister's boyfriend on the head with the biggest stick, he welcomes him and says congratulations when they announce their engagement.

'Could I go to your country if I wanted to?' I ask.

Joanna looks sad. 'I wish it was that easy.'

'Why don't you take all of us with you?' I say. 'Mama and Nyanbuot and my friends. Except we don't have money.'

'Juba, trust me, if I could, I would. But even if you had the money, the Immigration Department wouldn't be happy about it.'

'Is that the government? Would they be unhappy because there isn't enough food and space for everyone, like here in camp?' It's nice to think that the Australian government would care about that.

Joanna's face grows even glummer. 'Well, it's not that. It's more like . . . a policy.'

I'm not exactly sure what that is, but as it seems to make her sad I change the subject. 'I know one thing about Australia,' I say, remembering our class. 'Our teacher said it's right at the end of the world.'

Joanna smiles again at that. 'It's not really the end of the world, but it *is* called Down Under.'

'And do you have cows there too?'

'Yes,' she nods, 'plenty. So how many would you need to marry a Dinka girl?' Joanna looks at me and raises an eyebrow.

'Well . . . for the girl I have in mind, at least two hundred.'

'Really? Two hundred sounds like a lot. She must be a special girl.'

I smile as I think of Thiko. 'She is.'

Mama is excited when she sees that Joanna has come. She shakes her hand, pumping it up and down so hard I worry she'll hurt her. We sit together among the mess of the tent, me in the middle so I can translate. Mama says she wishes she'd gone to school when she was young so she could have learned to speak English.

'It's never too late to learn,' Joanna says, and I say it in Dinka to Mama. 'And speaking of learning, part of the reason I wanted to come and see you was to tell you in person how impressed I am with Juba. How helpful he's been, how quickly he's caught on. He's made my job a lot easier. Even better, he's good with the patients, and that's something that can't be taught. You either have that quality or you don't.' Joanna beams at me.

It's weird to translate that, but I do, and Mama's smile just grows bigger and wider.

Joanna stays a little longer to chat and once she's gone I hurry over to Thiko's tent. Luckily she's there. I gesture to her to come outside and we walk a little.

Then I slide the can of Coke out from under my shirt. 'Take a sip of this.'

She looks at me curiously, and when she tastes it her face changes completely. 'Delicious!' she exclaims. 'So sweet!' She takes another sip and burps loudly, just like I did, and falls into a similar state of giggles.

I let her drink the rest of the can, and when she's finished she says, 'Juba, that was amazing. How kind you are to share that.' She stops walking and holds my gaze as she reaches up and gently places a hand on my cheek.

I feel almost paralysed, but in a good way. There's nowhere else I would rather be at this moment. But I don't know what to do with my hands, or where to look. My eyes dart here and there, finally landing back on Thiko's face, and just as they do she steps all the way into me and stands on her tiptoes. Our lips meet.

My heart lurches. I've never kissed a girl before. It's the most wonderful feeling. The air tastes sweeter and fresher, as if a flower is blooming on my tongue. I am lightheaded when we pull apart.

'That,' I say softly, leaning my forehead against hers.

'That what?'

'That's what I've been wanting to ask you.'

She laughs. 'Really? But that wasn't a question. That was a kiss.'

I take her hands and stand there looking at her. My heart has melted and expanded all at the same time, and the breeze is running through my veins, my lungs, filling me with calm. We might be living in a refugee camp but right now, just for this moment, it feels like home.

And I make a promise to myself. One day I will live in a proper home again. With Mama and Nyanbuot and Thiko, and Chieng and Majok and the others. I will find Deng. And we'll all be together. Though we can't be sure what the next day will bring here, that is my promise.

Acknowledgements

Although it's my name on the cover of this book, there are many energetic people behind the scenes who worked very hard to make it the best it can be. I would like to thank the team at Penguin for believing in *When Elephants Fight* and supporting me in sharing it with the world. In particular, my wonderful publisher, Ben Ball: thank you for making 2018 the year of the elephants. Thank you also to the dynamic sales and marketing team.

It was a privilege to work with the best of the best editors, Meredith Rose, who read a thousand versions of this story with thoughtfulness and care. Her passion and sympathetic and insightful knowledge made working with her a great pleasure. Words will never express my gratitude for the faith she showed in Juba's journey. I would also like to thank my wonderful literary agent, Cheryl Akle, who championed this novel from start to finish.

I am very grateful for a grant from the Australia Council for the Arts that enabled me to complete this novel.